Bedfordshire Clanger Calamity

Albert Smith's Culinary Capers

Recipe 4

Steve Higgs

Dedication

To the makers of traditional British dishes wherever they may be.

Table of Contents:

Earl Hubert Bacon stared down at the man kneeling before him. 'What do you mean, you can't bake?' he enquired, already bored that he had to speak with the man at all. He didn't wish to converse with those he saved; they were here to perform tasks in exchange for surviving the coming apocalypse.

'I'm just the owner,' the kneeling man managed to stammer, somehow making the words sound like an apology.

The earl continued to stare down, anger making his nostrils flare. 'You expect me to believe that you own the Biggleswade Clanger Café and you cannot make the dish for which your business is famous. Utter poppycock, man! I have no time for this nonsense. Go into the kitchen and make me a perfect clanger right now and I shall put this unnecessary distraction down to the stress of travel.'

'Travel!' the man almost choked. 'You had me kidnapped!'

The earl raised one eyebrow. 'I saved you from the coming apocalypse, dear fellow. You should be thanking me, not messing me around by pretending you cannot bake.'

'He can't bake, boss.' The comment came from the man standing just behind and to the right of the man on his knees. He wore combat fatigues because he was ex-Army and thought it added a menacing look that his partner's choice of shirt, tie, and jacket failed to evoke.

The earl shifted his gaze up to look at the man who spoke and eyed him sceptically. 'Which one are you again?'

'Francis,' said Francis, sighing internally and questioning whether their boss refused to remember their names on purpose. 'He can't bake. We've

1

been in the kitchen with him for the last hour. He didn't even know there were different types of flour.' The earl's eyes flared in disbelief as he switched from looking at his henchman – he liked to think of them as henchmen – to the face looking up at him from the carpet. 'Eugene can bake better than this guy,' he referred to his well-dressed partner, secretly throwing some banter his way because Eugene's kitchen skills stopped at making a sandwich.

'Hey!' complained Eugene, standing to the left of the man on his knees.

Earl Bacon raised a hand to silence them both. They were chattering fools, amusing themselves with banalities and worthless pursuits. However, he had no stomach for violence and refused to leave the bunker unless it was absolutely necessary. His proclivities made the henchmen indispensable. When they fell silent, he pursed his lips and once again stared down at the man kneeling by his feet.

'You really cannot bake?' he asked, his voice filled with disappointment.

Sensing his ordeal might be about to come to an end, the man snatched at what he thought was the lifeline he'd been thrown. 'No. Not one bit. Can I go now?'

'Go?' Earl Bacon thought it an odd request. 'Well, I suppose I have no further use for you. Tell me though, before my employees escort you out, who is it that I should have rescued in your stead? Who at the Biggleswade Clanger Café can bake me a perfect clanger?'

Wondering if he might be safe to get to his feet, Joel Clement, the owner of the Clanger Café, slid a foot around to get it under his body and watched to see if anyone would stop him. Wary enough to keep his hands open and out in a submissive surrender pose, he stood up. 'There are four

2

chefs that know the recipe. They have all worked for me for years now. Any one of them could show you how to do it. We run a class twice a week. I could arrange a special VIP event just for you and your ... friends?' he suggested hopefully. The moment he got away from these lunatics and found out where they'd taken him, he was going to call the police, but he was going to say anything he could think of to keep them calm until then.

The earl gasped at the ridiculous suggestion. 'No, no, no, that won't do at all. Everyone on the surface will be dead soon. I have explained this to you already. Travel is unthinkable. Who is your best chef? I want that person.'

Joel swallowed nervously. Whoever he named would be their next victim. Who should he pick? The answer to the madman's question was Victor Harris. He was easily the best chef. He made the clangers more neatly and more swiftly than anyone else. When Victor started eight years ago, he reorganised the entire kitchen, making it streamlined and efficient, which allowed Joel to naturally waste off two staff from the kitchen, saving him a packet. Victor also brought his sister along to work in the shop and it hadn't taken Joel long to fall for her alluring looks and long legs. No, he couldn't give them Victor's name, Kate would never forgive him. How about April? She was his oldest member of staff and could be a vicious-tongued cow when she wanted to be.

'I do not like to be made to wait,' growled Earl Bacon, prompting Joel to spit out a name.

'Maddie Hayes!' he blurted, wondering where he got the name from at the last moment. It was completely made up, the idea to lie and give them a false name coming to him only when the words were forming on his lips.

'Maddie Hayes,' repeated Hubert slowly.

'Yes. She's easily my best,' Joel nodded enthusiastically, selling the false name so he could finish this insane experience and escape.

'Very well ...' The earl had been about to address the café owner by name but realised he hadn't bothered to learn it. Other people held no interest for him. Unless they were one of the greats who had produced a food worthy of his attention, they were little more than ants scurrying about on the pavement beneath his feet. Not that he could see the pavement or his feet. Years of overindulgence had seen to that. Waist size was another trifling insignificance though; he lived to be well-fed, and only ate the finest foods, or those treats he felt worthy of his attention. The clanger was one such treat. He'd savoured his first one on an excursion with his father many years before. Back when his father was Earl Bacon, he would travel the country on hunting and fishing trips, the father taking the son most everywhere he went. A gurgle from his belly reminded him that he needed to wrap up this business. 'Very well, you are of no further use. Please dispose of him,' the final request was aimed at his henchmen, Eugene and Francis.

The order jolted Joel. 'Dispose? What do you mean dispose? You said I could go!'

Eugene frowned in surprise. 'Did I? Well, I suppose you can go, in a way. I can't return you home though. You cannot bake therefore you have no purpose.'

Joel could see the two men to his rear moving forward. The one in army dress had a short piece of rope in his hands! 'Who are you?' he squealed at the earl.

It was a question he'd been asked before by the people he chose to save. He relished being asked it because it gave him a chance to deliver his favourite line. 'Me? Why, I'm the bad guy.'

Albert was beginning to get the impression something was wrong. He couldn't work out what it was, but the people working in the shop, the man who taught the class he attended, and the chefs working in the kitchen behind the counter, were all acting as if there was a massive elephant in the room. He could see them verbally stepping around it.

His class, the first of his trip to pass without incident, had been a revelation. He didn't even know you could make puff pastry; he thought a person had to buy it in blocks from the supermarket and that it was made in a giant machine somewhere. He'd rolled out, filled, closed, crimped, and baked his wonderful clanger and then sat down in the café to eat the whole thing. At almost eighteen inches long, it was more food than he needed but he wasn't going to let a crumb go to waste.

Customers in the class got to select their filling from the full range the shop offered. He chose pork with sage and cider for his savoury end and rhubarb with custard for the sweet end. Both halves were sublime but, truth be told, he preferred the savoury fillings, only making two-courses-in-one in the class because tradition demanded it.

As he finished off the last few crumbs, Albert lifted the empty plate to show his dog, Rex Harrison. Rex, a former police dog, fired for his terrible attitude towards his human handlers and their malfunctioning noses, narrowed his eyes disapprovingly at the plate.

Albert rolled his eyes. 'You already ate yours,' he pointed out. 'You didn't need mine as well.'

Rex had been waiting patiently for his human to offer him whatever was left on his plate. Cleaning plates was one of his specialities and a service he provided regularly because his human's appetite rarely extended to encompass everything he'd been served. His own clanger barely touched the sides on its way down.

To show his thoughts on the matter, since his human was terrible at understanding what Rex had to say, he flopped heavily to the cool floor tile with a grumpy harrumph. That was until a sniggering sound drew his attention. From a gap beneath a waist-high swing door in the counter, a nose protruded.

Rex had caught the scent of the other dog the moment they entered the establishment, but this was the first time he'd seen him. It was a dachshund, an odd-shaped dog in Rex's opinion. He was indifferent to it, much as he was most dogs, but his neutral opinion shifted gear because it seemed to be taking pleasure in seeing Rex denied his human's meal.

'What's your problem?' he growled quietly, lifting his head to give the small dog a warning glare.

A hand touched his head, his human stroking his fur. 'Settle down, Rex,' Albert chided. Albert hadn't spotted the sausage dog behind the counter, nor could he decipher its smell over all the other scents in the café. Not that he used his nose to gather information. Like all humans, he relied on sight and sound and was unaware that ignoring his most informative sense annoyed his dog. His attention wasn't on Rex and whatever he might be growling at, it was on the young lady working behind the counter.

She was average height with light brown hair that looked like it couldn't decide whether to be blond or brunette. Her face was a little pinched and her nose a little long. Basically, she was a little plain-looking but that wasn't the dominant thing he noticed. Above all else, she looked sad. Or possibly worried, Albert thought. He knew nothing of her or her situation, so it could be that the tension he could perceive was nothing

7

more than a workplace disagreement. Maybe she turned up late for work and was on her final warning. For what was probably the fifth time, he told himself to stop looking at her and mind his own business.

Their accommodation was a short walk away along Hitching Road where Albert's daughter Selina had booked him into Ye Old Leather Bottle, a public house with a restaurant that boasted a Michelin star. It was now late on a Tuesday afternoon on his second day in Biggleswade, a delightful small town in Bedfordshire. He arrived feeling wary for what unwelcome surprise the town might hold for him – the last three stops on his culinary tour of the British Isles had each presented murder and mayhem. He wanted a nice quiet couple of days in Bedfordshire to recover, but almost thirty hours after arriving, he was wondering if perhaps he might be feeling a little bored.

Rex couldn't decide whether to turn his back on the annoying dachshund, a demonstration of how unbothered he was by the tiny dog, or to just lunge forward and scare the laugh out of him. His lead was looped around the foot of his human's chair, a needless precaution in Rex's opinion because if he wanted to go, the chair leg would either snap, or just flip the chair over, and if he didn't want to go, a simple request from his human would keep him in place. He'd demonstrated this to be true recently, throwing his human to the carpet in a bid to get to a piece of bacon. His human appeared to be upset by the event for many hours afterward, but Rex got the bacon and that was what counted.

The dachshund looked set to say something else, but before he could, a human hand looped under his belly and the four tiny feet Rex could see under the bottom of the swing door, vanished from sight as he was lifted into the air. Appearing again in a female human's arms, the dog acted as if being carried around was a privilege bestowed upon him and not an embarrassing indication of just how small he was. No human would try to carry Rex: he weighed the same as a large man.

Albert looked up from checking his phone when someone approached his table. It was the lady from behind the counter, the one who looked sad. Was it his imagination? Or was it a brave smile she wore?

'Are you all done here?' she asked, glancing to his plate which quite clearly had nothing but crumbs remaining on it.

'Yes, thank you,' Albert replied. The dachshund was balanced along her left forearm with its butt end tucked under her armpit. It leaned forward to smell Albert. 'Cute dachshund,' he said, striking up a conversation. 'What's his name?'

The woman smiled as she glanced down at her dog and back up. The smile reached her eyes for the first time since Albert had started observing her. 'This is Hans. He's my little bratwurst!' she exclaimed in an over-excited manner while jiggling the dog to make his ears flap.

Albert didn't react or turn his head when the bell tinkled to signal that the café door had just opened. It was behind him, and he was still watching the woman's face. It was because he was watching her face and not turning to look at whoever might be coming in that he saw the blood drain from the woman's cheeks. Her smile fell away, and she staggered slightly, putting a hand out to grip the back of the chair opposite Albert for support.

Thinking she might fall – she really looked that close to passing out – Albert got to his feet. 'Are you alright, my dear?' he enquired, glancing across the shop where he spied two uniformed officers accompanying a man in a suit and coat. He knew a plain-clothes policeman when he saw one; they all looked the same somehow.

'I'm … I.' The woman couldn't form a coherent sentence but managed to pull the spare chair out so she could collapse into it. The police went to the counter where they were met by a stern-looking woman. 'It's my Joel,' the woman now sitting at Albert's table sobbed quietly. 'He went missing three days ago, and …' she sobbed, tears filling her eyes, 'and they found his body yesterday morning. It was in Wales. What on Earth was he doing in Wales? I filed the missing person report just before they found his body, but they said he'd been murdered.' She gasped suddenly. 'They must be here to tell me they caught the killer!'

At the counter, the stern-faced woman nodded her head and narrowed her eyes before jutting out an arm. 'That's her sitting there,' she told the plain-clothes police officer. Albert was looking her way but didn't understand her expression: she looked pleased to be pointing the police to the woman at his table, but not in a good way.

His natural instinct was to take the woman's hand for support even though he didn't know her. She looked wretched already, but he resisted temptation, curious to hear what the officer in charge might be about to say. He was approaching now, the two uniformed officers filing along behind.

'Kate Harris?' the lead officer sought to confirm, taking out his identification to show her.

'Yes,' she replied nervously.

Rex lifted his head. There was something going on. His human talking to other humans was of little interest unless they were also preparing food, in which case he would watch them like a hawk ready for dropped ingredients – anything that touched the floor was his. However, he could smell the woman sitting at their table with the annoying little sausage dog was upset, and that made him curious. More than that though, there was a big piece of clanger under one of the tables by the window. If the police created a distraction, it was going to be his.

'I am Detective Sergeant Craig. Kate Harris can you account for your whereabouts on Saturday night?'

She blinked up at the detective. 'What?'

'You filed a missing person report in which you stated that you arrived home at approximately 1900hrs expecting to find your boyfriend Joel Clement already there. You stated that you waited up for him and made several phone calls, but he failed to appear at any point that night. Did you stay at home throughout Saturday night?'

She blinked again, confused by the question. 'Yes,' she replied, the word coming slowly as if she questioned whether it was the right answer to give.

Albert knew what was going on. He'd been the detective asking these questions many times himself.

The detective pressed her with his next question. 'Can you provide anyone who can confirm that you stayed in the house all night?'

'Someone who can confirm … why?' The tears had stopped and now Kate Harris just looked confused.

'Just answer the question, please, Miss Harris. The officers who came to your house found blood on the floor in the kitchen.'

'Joel hit his head on the oven extractor. I told them that,' Kate protested.

The detective narrowed his eyes. 'Can you provide a reliable alibi for your whereabouts on Saturday night?' The detective's voice was flat and calm. He was just doing his job, neither deriving pleasure from it, nor loathing that it was his job to do.

'Alibi.' The word slipped out on a hushed breath as around the café, staff and customers were all utterly silent to hear what was being said.

With a nod to the two uniformed officers, DS Craig decided he had enough to proceed. 'Kate Harris I am arresting you on suspicion of the murder of Joel Clement.'

'What!' Kate physically jerked at the suggestion she was responsible for her boyfriend's murder.

The detective sergeant carried on despite her interruption. 'You do not have to say anything, but it may harm your defence if you do not mention when questioned something you later rely on in court. Anything you do say may be given in evidence.'

Sitting less than a foot from where Albert was standing, Kate was sobbing uncontrollably now. Albert had no idea who Joel Clement might be or what might have befallen him, other than he had been murdered, and he had no reason to doubt that the police had evidence that linked the murder to the woman. However, a lifetime – roughly six decades – of thinking like a detective, told him they were off the mark this time.

Respecting the uniform, he took a step back as the two junior men moved in to physically arrest Kate Harris.

'I didn't do it!' Kate wailed. 'Why would I hurt him? I loved him!' she was struggling to get the words out and her makeup was a mess.

Albert knew the officers would have to cuff her. It was standard practice and the only safe way to manage a person once arrested. He remembered many occasions when his cases led him to do exactly the same. Nevertheless, her reaction looked real not faked – she hadn't killed Joel Clement.

The first uniformed officer to touch her, went for her right arm, but she jerked and attempted to snatch it away, succeeding in breaking his grip. 'I said I didn't do it!' she yelled, emotion overcoming her. Her dog was still tucked under her left arm, and now the situation was becoming dangerous and difficult.

The detective sergeant, who blocked her route from the shop, raised his voice to say, 'Move back, please, sir.' It was clearly aimed at Albert who hadn't moved and was trying to decide what his course of action ought to be. He couldn't intervene, that would be wrong, and the officers would be right to arrest him were he to do so. However, he also felt unhappy to do nothing.

Kate cried out in anguish and twisted away again, shouting, 'Stop it! Leave me alone!'

The customers in the shop were all staring at the incident, and the ruckus had drawn the staff from the kitchen to gather behind the counter where they now stood and gawped. Albert heard one ask, 'What's going on?'

The reply came from the stern-faced woman who was smiling when she said, 'Kate killed Joel. I always said she was nothing but a gold digger.'

Still weeping, Kate had nowhere to go and the three officers had done an effective job of pinning her in place until she calmed down. Albert liked that they hadn't gone down the route of using force to arrest her. 'You're really going to arrest me?' sobbed Kate, looking dazed and bewildered.

They didn't need to answer; she already knew that they were. Confused by what was happening to her, she turned to look at Albert and thrust her little dog into his arms. 'Look after him, please,' she begged. The cops were just about to put the cuffs on her when someone vaulted the counter.

It was a man in his early thirties, and he was royally angry. 'Hey!' he bellowed. 'Take your hands off her! What's the meaning of this?'

Demonstrating the seasoned nature of his career, the DS Craig swivelled around to face the new threat. 'Stay back, sir. This person is under arrest for the murder of Joel Clement.'

'Don't be so absurd,' the man snapped in reply. He wore chef's whites and a hair net, but it was his face that stole Albert's attention; there were facial resemblances between his features and Kate's, and he was willing to bet they were siblings.

DS Craig wasn't in a mood to be messed about. 'Stand back, sir. Or I shall have you arrested for obstructing me in the course of my duties.'

'You are not taking my sister,' the man growled. 'She hasn't done anything wrong.' Albert closed his eyes and sighed. It was the wrong thing to do. Even if the police had this all wrong, challenging them now, and so directly, was foolhardy.

'Take her to the car,' snapped DS Craig, essentially challenging Kate's brother to stop them. When the officers moved, each holding one of Kate's arms, the detective stared at the chef effectively daring him to intervene.

Albert thought he was going to and breathed a genuine sigh of relief when the brother made the right decision and backed down.

When the café door closed, the people inside could still see the police and their suspect through the windows which dominated the entire front aspect of the building. It was deathly silent inside until the stern-faced woman said, 'Get back to work, the lot of you. Nobody's paying you to gawp.'

The staff didn't move though, not immediately. Most of those Albert could see were looking at the brother. He appeared to still be debating going after his sister, but upon hearing the stern-faced woman's orders, he spun around to challenge her instead. 'Who do you think you are, April? You're not in charge.'

His response was quickly followed by a woman standing behind the counter, whose meek voice wanted to know, 'Is anybody paying us at all now?' Her question stopped everyone in their tracks. 'They just arrested Kate for Mr Clement's murder. If the owner of the café is dead, what does that mean for the rest of us.'

Now that his eyes were drawn to the huddle of staff behind the counter, Albert saw just how upset most of them looked. The split between men and women was about even, and the age range ran from teenagers up to three people who looked to be in their mid-sixties. The stern-faced woman was one of the oldest. Albert counted twelve staff in total. Their conversation became a mess of noise as everyone spoke over the top of everyone else.

Watching them, Albert wrinkled his nose as he thought about what he wanted to do. He was still holding the woman's dog and needed to give it to someone before he left but he was currently in no hurry to do so. He was also in no hurry to leave and though he was booked to stay for only one more night in Biggleswade, he knew the pub wasn't fully booked if he chose to stay.

Stroking the dachshund absentmindedly, the sound of a chair being dragged across the tiled floor brought his attention crashing back to his own dog. 'Rex!' he yelled as he looked about for the large German Shepherd. Rex was not where he'd been left, and nor was Albert's chair which was weaving between tables on its way to the window.

Ha! Got you! thought Rex, pouncing on the forgotten piece of pastry with glee. His human could disapprove all he wanted now that it had been swallowed.

Albert caught up to his great brute of a dog, grabbing his collar and yanking his head out from under a table. They were right over by the door, his dog under a table at which two men sat.

'Sorry about that,' mumbled Albert, getting nothing but a stiff nod in response. Albert dragged his dog away, Rex letting him as he licked his lips joyously. Neither Albert nor Rex intended to notice the two men, truthfully neither of them really did, but their brains logged their details anyway.

They were on the large side, both in height and girth, but the girth was mostly muscle, honed from many hours in the gym. They were dressed very differently, one in a smart grey jacket, with a white shirt and plain dark grey tie. His trousers were black, the effect of his outfit making him look like someone who succeeded in life and needed to dress smartly to meet clients or customers but had no need to wear a suit. Opposite him, drinking tea from a small china cup, his pinky finger extended as he lifted it to his mouth, the second man wore combat fatigues as if he were an extra from a war movie.

Rex recorded them not by their appearance but by their smell, his nose sifting and sorting constantly whether he wanted it to or not. Neither man nor dog realised at the time how significant that early encounter would prove.

Rex wanted to remain ambiguous to the dachshund, but found he genuinely felt sorry for the little guy.

'What's happening?' the little guy asked, thoroughly confused by the sudden absence of his human, especially given the circumstances of her departure, and how upset she had been.

'She was taken away by the police,' Rex replied. 'Did she hurt someone?'

The dachshund spun through a hundred and eighty degrees, baring his teeth, and growling with a deep snarl. 'Don't you cast dispersions on my human! I'll ... I'll ... I'll take your leg off and beat you to death with it you oversized, one-step-removed-from-a-wolf-looking pile of poop! My human wouldn't hurt anyone.'

Rex's eyebrows shifted in mute surprise. 'You have a lot of attitude for someone who looks like they were designed to be eaten in a bun.'

Hans, already bewildered by current events, darted forward to bite Rex's ankle. He got scooped by Albert though who had no idea what all the noise was about but didn't think adding a dog fight to the mix was a great idea.

His face still like thunder, Kate's brother crossed the café to get her dog. His expression changed while he walked, the man taking a deep breath and forcing his tense shoulders to relax. Just before he got to Albert, he paused and turned to face the room. 'I'm terribly sorry about all that, folks,' he addressed the customers, not one of whom had chosen to leave. 'The police have made a mistake, obviously. However, the incident interrupted your afternoon so please all come to the counter

17

before you leave and take a free clanger home as an apology. One per person, any size you like.'

'Hey, you can't do that,' argued April, her stern-face looking even stonier now.

Kate's brother just ignored her. 'One per person, anything you like.' With his back firmly to the mean-spirited older lady, he gave Albert an apologetic smile. 'Thank you for stepping in to take Hans. I think Kate would have been doubly upset if they'd taken him away too.'

Albert inclined his head in acknowledgement as he handed Hans over, and said, 'Terrible business.' When Kate's brother lifted an eyebrow, he added, 'The murder, I mean. I overheard that it was the owner who died. He was your sister's … partner?' he tried, not sure what the correct term might be now that no one seemed to get married any more. Albert was prying – something he did naturally, though he couldn't now tell if he did it because he'd been a policeman for so long, or if he'd always done it and that was what made him such a good policeman. However, his question made the other man's eyebrows shoot for the sky. 'I used to be a detective before I got old.' Albert explained.

Albert's statement seemed to quell the rising surprise at his question. 'A detective? So you know about this sort of thing? What will happen to Kate now? How long will it take them to work out that they have the wrong person?'

It was a barrage of questions, but Albert didn't need to be anywhere other than where he was. Rex had enjoyed plenty of exercise today and there was little left on his agenda other than to read a book, get some supper, and maybe enjoy a gin before bed.

'Do you have a few minutes?' Albert asked, indicating the table and chairs with his hand.

18

Kate's brother glanced at the clock; it was close to closing time. There was no more baking to do today. He'd worked a long shift, coming in early to make the pastry fresh this morning at five o'clock but the tasks he still ought to perform could wait a while. He took the chair Kate had used to keep herself upright and deposited Hans the dachshund on his lap as the old man sat opposite.

Rex sat upright, his head appearing above the table where his tongue lolled out to drip drool to the tile below. He eyed the dachshund suspiciously, his attention rewarded by bared teeth again as the tiny dog made another silent threat. Rex chose to ignore him.

Albert extended his hand. 'I'm Albert Smith. Formerly Detective Superintendent Smith.'

The action caught Victor off guard: he'd forgotten his manners and it hadn't occurred to him to introduce himself. 'Sorry, I'm Victor Harris, Kate's brother, but I guess you figured that part out from all the shouting.'

Albert nodded and moved on. Taking a few minutes to answer the man's initial list of questions by explaining the process of being arrested and processed. His words filled the man with horror.

'But she didn't do it,' he protested needlessly.

Albert pursed his lips and drew a slow breath in through his nose. 'The police clearly believe they have reason to think otherwise. They would not arrest her without cause.'

'How can you be so sure?' Victor asked carefully. He wanted to rail and rage at anyone who would listen, but the kindly old man was giving freely of his time and he had to respect that.

19

It was an obvious question, and one Albert had been asked many times in the past. The answer was almost always the same. 'The police have too little time to allow any of it to go to waste. They discovered the body when exactly?'

Victor's eyes rolled to the top of their sockets as he searched the memory part of his brain. 'They let Kate know two days ago on Sunday night. She called me moments later in a flood of tears. I don't know what she was thinking turning up to work today, but she stayed home yesterday and today said she didn't want to be in their house all by herself with nothing to do but wallow.' Remembering the question, he added, 'They told her his body was found Sunday morning.'

Albert nodded along as Victor laid out the little that he knew. Joel Clement, the owner of the Biggleswade Clanger Café had failed to come home after work on Saturday. He lived with Kate in her small terraced house, but sometimes went to the pub on his way home. Often this was with Kate, but not on that occasion as Kate had a Pilates class. She arrived home after the class, expecting to find Joel there waiting for her. On her way, she picked up a takeaway meal from a supermarket to cook for them both, but he wasn't there, and he didn't come home at any point that evening. According to Victor, his sister claimed it to be the first time Joel had ever done such a thing and she was mightily angry with him for staying out all night and ruining their Saturday evening. She suspected he'd had a skin-full and crashed somewhere else, muttering that if he'd gotten so drunk he'd gone home with another woman, he'd be staying somewhere else for the rest of his life.

When he failed to appear looking sheepish and hungover at work the next morning, Kate began to get concerned. She started calling around to people she knew he knew, asking if anyone had seen him. Kate even excused herself from work to go to the pub he frequented at lunchtime that day to see what they could tell her. The report from the landlord was that Joel had been in, he was a regular and easily recognised, but he left after just two pints. Once the landlord assured her he left alone and had been reading a paper and using his phone rather than talking to anyone, she began to let genuine worry creep in.

Where was he? The end of the working day came around and he was still not answering his phone. No one knew where he could be, and Kate had run out of people to ask. Almost. Dreading the task, she drove to his ex-wife's house and knocked on the door.

Albert had questions about why Joel lived in Kate's house, when Victor described it as a small terraced house. Surely, as a successful business owner, he must be making decent money and be able to afford a nice house. Of course, a person can choose to spend their money however they wish, but it didn't sound right to Albert's ears, and he had planned to ask for more detail. Now he didn't need to. Joel left his wife for Kate. It sounded like a terrible thing to do, especially when Victor revealed that the couple had two teenage children.

'How old is Joel?' Albert asked, thinking he must be a decade or more older than Kate who looked to be around twenty-five.

'Thirty-nine,' replied Victor. 'He looks older if I'm being honest. He hasn't taken great care of himself but he's a great guy and Kate clearly loves him. They hit it off when Kate took a job here. I was already working in the kitchen when a role came up in the café. She trained as an accountant but hated the firm she worked for. It was one of those catch twenty-two situations where she needed the job but hated the job and had no reason to believe a job at a different firm would be any different. I only suggested she work alongside me on a whim, but she knew I loved working here and she quit her old job the next day. That was two years ago.'

Albert listened to everything, absorbing information like a sponge. The infidelity grated against his beliefs, but he kept his mouth shut: he had no right to sit in judgement even if he did think it loathsome for a man to walk out on his wife and children when a younger woman showed some interest. 'You were telling me Kate went to see Joel's ex-wife,' Albert prompted.

'Yes. I don't know what she was thinking. It went badly as you can imagine, and Trisha hadn't heard from Joel of course. She's not a very nice person, truth be told. Nor are his children. She cleaned him out in the divorce, took everything but the shop and she wanted that too. He managed to keep hold of it by giving her everything else – you know what divorce lawyers are like.'

He didn't, actually. Albert married once and loved Petunia as deeply as a man could. It would never have occurred to him to leave her or mess her around. It wasn't germane to the case though, and he shifted the conversation forward rather than comment. 'What evidence against her might there be?' he asked. 'The police confirmed she has no alibi for the time of his disappearance and for the period when he is believed to have been killed.'

'Wait,' Victor frowned. 'I didn't hear them ask her about when he was killed.'

That's because they hadn't. 'She reported him missing, yes?'

'Yes.'

Albert scrunched up his face, needing to deliver some bad news and wondering how best to do it. 'You would not believe the number of times the person reporting a person as missing is the one responsible for the murder.' Victor's eyes flared in surprise and he sat more upright as he started to bristle. Albert held up a hand to calm the younger man. 'I'm not saying that is the case here, but the police will not take the fact that she filed the report into account. They may even consider it a point against her. They asked her where she was at a specific time; that will be the time the coroner has estimated to be the time of death. She has no alibi; therefore, she could be Joel's killer.'

'That's ridiculous,' Victor spluttered. 'She loved him. I have been waiting for her to announce their engagement.' Albert had dealt with this so many times in the past. For family members and close friends, the idea that the person they knew could be guilty of such a heinous crime was unthinkable and nothing would shake their conviction.

Albert asked. 'What did she have to gain?'

'To gain?' echoed Victor.

'The whole shop,' said a loud voice from behind the counter. Both men turned their heads to see April glaring their way. 'That's right,' she snapped. 'He named her as a partner in the business.' Her announcement got the attention of everyone in the café; customers and staff alike. 'What? She didn't tell you?' asked April with mock surprise. 'They didn't tell anyone. I only know because I saw it on Companies House. She has an equal share of the business. Fifty percent is his, and fifty percent is hers. I told you she was a gold-digger!' she made a point of reminding everyone. 'It didn't take her long to bump him off, did it? I bet the ink on her signature wasn't even dry before she wrapped the rope around his neck.'

One of the other women behind the counter cried out in revulsion at the mental image, but Victor was on his feet and his face looked like a volcano about to erupt. 'You'd better shut your mouth, April. Or so help me ...'

'What?' she laughed in his face. 'You'll bump me off? Like sister like brother. Some family, aren't they?' she shared her joke with the rest of

23

the staff, not that any of them thought it funny. Cutting him off before he could say anymore, she spun around and started walking toward the door that led from the counter area to whatever lay beyond in the rear of the premises. 'If you don't mind, someone needs to do the books now that Miss Homewrecker isn't here. Maybe we'll be able to keep our jobs if someone steps up to manage this place properly now.' It was quite clear from her comment that she was referring to herself in the role of manager, taking the post because there was no one to appoint her. The door swung shut behind her before anyone could do anything to argue.

Albert tilted his head and thought about all that he had seen and heard in the last half an hour. It was a curious set of circumstances.

Rex was curious too. Curious enough to try talking to the angry dachshund. 'Hey, Weiner,' he chuffed at the dog. Hans was back on the floor, unceremoniously dumped there when Victor sprang to his feet to fight with April.

Hans turned his head slowly to look at the German Shepherd. He wasn't a fan of large dogs. They all thought size was the only factor that mattered and this one looked like he'd been cross bred with a bear. 'My name is Hans,' he growled.

'Okay, Hans. My human is what passes for clever among humans. He might be able to help with what is going on. Have you smelled anything new or unusual near your territory?'

Hans tilted his head and narrowed his eyes. 'What are you? A police dog?'

'Yes, actually. I used to be anyway. My human was a police officer.'

'Like those humans that took my human away?' growled Hans. 'You expect me to trust you? You look like a big dumb brute to me. Getting my human back is going to take brains not brawn. Leave the detective work to me, you don't look qualified. I'll let you know if I need someone to pee really high up on a lamppost.'

Rex frowned at the small dog but wouldn't let himself rise to the bait.

Albert had run out of reasons to stay in the café. Most of the customers had already left, put off by the ugly display by April so soon after the unpleasant scenes with the police. A few had taken up Victor's offer of a free clanger, but most just left, their hunger already sated and the desire to leave greater than the draw of free food.

Only two men remained, the two Albert had to apologise to when Rex went under their table to get a flake of food. He didn't feel his conversation with Victor had ended – he certainly had more questions he wanted answers to, but this wasn't his investigation, he wasn't a serving police officer, and it was very possible that they already had the right person in custody.

With a quick shake of Rex's lead, Albert got himself moving toward the door. Victor ran after him.

'Mr Smith,' he called.

'Albert will do.'

'Albert, I just wanted to thank you for your time. You came in for the class, didn't you? I hope this hasn't spoiled the experience. It's always such a pleasure for us to share our craft with others. The clanger has such a fine tradition in these parts.'

'It was what brought me all the way here, Victor. It's getting late though; I think I'll be off. I hope your sister is proven to be innocent.' It was a throwaway statement, a thing to say as he went out the door.

By his knee, Rex was sniffing the air near the two men sitting in the window. He had no reason to do so, but much like a human has to always be looking at something, so a dog must always be sniffing and sorting smells. He filed away the various scents, categorising and memorising as he always did without conscious thought about why or how.

His lead went taut: his human was already outside on the pavement and looking to move away. A light drizzle had set in, which pleased Rex not one bit. Nor the sniggering that came from behind as Hans made a clever remark about moving along like a good boy. The dachshund said, 'Good boy,' with more emphasis than was necessary to drive his point home. Rex almost spun around to growl a reply but acted instead as if he hadn't heard. If he got the chance, he was going to accidentally pee on the annoying dog's head.

Albert got about halfway to the pub before he changed his mind about interfering.

The rain was picking up by the time Albert turned around. He'd been trying to convince himself that he would have a nice, quiet, and above all pleasant evening reading a book in the pub. He could relax in his room for a while and maybe get a bath. Rex didn't need dinner because he'd just eaten an entire eighteen inch long clanger, but the dog would have forgotten about that by the time they arrived at the pub and stare at his bowl because Rex's body clock would assure him it was dinner time.

Keeping the dog away from his dinner bowl to avoid an hour or more of grumpy dog noises wasn't what caused the u-turn. It wasn't even the acknowledgement that the pub would be filled with young people making noise and playing the fruit machine and jukebox. Despite telling himself a quiet evening was what he desired, truthfully, he wanted to find out if the woman he met earlier really killed her lover.

Because he didn't believe she had.

He'd seen her face when DS Craig arrested her. More importantly, he'd seen her eyes. She had no idea why the police would accuse her and that made her innocent: Albert was sure of it. A homewrecker she might be, but that wasn't a crime in the eyes of the law. If April was right, and Kate had just inherited the entire café, the police would consider that to be a strong motive. They might take the stance that she seduced the older man as the first stage in a cold-hearted plan to murder him and take the café. There were many recorded cases of worse behaviour. However, if Albert's instincts were right, the poor woman might be tried and found guilty of a crime she hadn't committed while the true killer went free.

It would keep him awake all night if he didn't at least explore what might have happened.

Arriving back at the café, he'd been forced to turn his collar up as the rain became persistent, but the door was now displaying a closed sign.

Rex hated the rain. He hated the way it bounced off his ears and how his paws flicked it up onto his belly where his coat was so short, he was virtually bald. The rain was cold and unwelcome and though it wouldn't penetrate his coat to reach his skin anywhere else, it would saturate the outer layer of fur and take hours to dry out. Generally, he was happy to go wherever his human chose to wander. The old man spent a lot of time going to different places, and there was always something to do, new smells to discover, and, quite often, something to eat.

Today, however, they had been out for hours and he was quite looking forward to going home. They were back at the café, which was okay by him; the café had food inside and it was right about dinner time according to the clock in his head.

Wondering why they were not going inside, he looked up at his human and got rewarded with a rain drop right on his nose, a portion of which whooshed right up his left nostril. He ducked his head again, using his left front leg to wipe at his face, and he sneezed, a spectacular explosion of dog snot and rainwater as his head spasmed.

Pulling an odd face as he tried to decide if he needed to sneeze again, Rex sniffed, and that was when he caught the scent. He held it in his nose, deciphering it. His human was moving, turning to his left and about to walk away, but Rex dug his feet in and leaned his bodyweight in the opposite direction. The smell meant something. It lingered on the air despite the rain damping everything down.

'Come along, Rex.' His human tugged at the lead, trying to make him budge but with little effect. 'What can you smell, boy?' The question meant his human was paying attention at least. The answer was that he could smell the men from the café, the ones who were sitting by the door. The combination of scents coming from the pair blended together to give him an unquestionable result. They were not in the café, he could see that, using his eyes for once in favour of his nose. He got to his feet and looked around, lifting his nose higher as he sucked in air and tried to pinpoint where the scent was coming from. He wasn't doing this for any particular reason, only because their scent was familiar and unexpected.

Behind him, Albert had moved position so he could see through the window into the back of the café. Beyond the counter, he could see someone moving around. The business shut for the day, but someone was working, and he hoped it might be Victor. Peering through the glass façade, he spotted Victor's face, which confirmed there was reason to knock on the window. The action startled the man inside, his surprised expression appearing in the round window of the kitchen door.

Moments later, Victor came through it, a question on his brow as he came to see who might be there.

The sound of the door locks clicking open distracted Rex before he could find the source of the scent he held. He would need to leave where he was to pursue the smell, but it looked like his human was going back inside the café.

'Hello again, Albert,' Victor held the door open with his left hand, clasping the frame with his right so he blocked the gap with his body as he leaned outside into the cool damp air. 'Did you leave something behind?' he glanced into the café. 'I didn't see anything.'

Albert bit his lip, wondering only now how he might make his suggestion. 'No, no, nothing like that. Actually, I wondered if I might be of assistance.'

Victor's eyebrows knitted together as he missed what the old man was saying. 'In the kitchen?' he tried to clarify.

Shaking his head quickly at his ambiguous choice of words, Albert had another go at explaining. 'No, I meant with your sister's situation.' He wasn't making himself clear if Victor's single raised eyebrow was anything to go by, so he stuffed his next sentence full of words. 'I'm something of an amateur sleuth, one might say. I've had some success in uncovering what the police may fail to even look for. You see, I saw your sister's face when they arrested her. I'm convinced that she is innocent, and I would like to help you prove it. Just in case the case against her holds water.'

Victor's expression was pained. He was trying to work out how to tell the old man to go home and stop wasting his time; he had enough on his plate without trying to solve the café owner's murder in his spare time. The business had no owner, April was trying to forcibly take over running the place, his own job was in jeopardy, and his sister was under arrest. What good could an old man do?

'I'm sorry,' he started to say, but just as he began to speak, the rain picked up, doubling in volume one second to the next. Rex decided enough was enough and barged his way past Victor's legs to get into the dry. Doing so dragged Albert along with him, the dog's strength easily enough to pull the old man off balance.

Albert let the lead slip from his hand rather than collide with Victor, but his dog was in the café now and about to shake all the excess water from his fur. Seeing this, but unable to get to him, Albert shouted, 'No, Rex!'

Rex heard the shout but couldn't imagine what it was his human didn't want him to do. He would find out once he'd lightened his coat some.

30

Victor watched in horror as a million droplets of muddy water showered the inside of his freshly cleaned café. Seat, tables, walls, the windows – they all got a coating as both he and Albert rushed to stop the dog.

Enjoying the blissful sensation of shaking his body, Rex was in the throes of working down to his tail when hands grabbed him. The unexpectedness made him jump, springing around to face the danger with his teeth bared.

Faced with a mouthful of giant teeth he didn't expect, Victor's instinctive reaction was to get away from them, but his sudden change in direction caused his feet to slip on the wet floor. He crashed to the tile, jarring his hip, but the dog wasn't following up with an attack and the old man seemed to have him under control.

Rex eyed the new human suspiciously. 'You're sitting in a puddle,' he observed.

As cold water soaked through the material of his trousers, Victor clambered back to his feet and looked about at the mess he would now have to clean up. Everyone else had gone home, even April, who argued with him about his plan to stay. She wanted him to hand over his key and claimed that someone was fiddling the books. When she said 'Someone' she made air quotes and made it quite clear the someone she meant was his sister Kate. Kate did the books, taking over from April at Joel's instruction six months ago. April had been the bookkeeper as one of her duties since before Joel bought the shop more than a decade ago, but Kate was qualified as an accountant which meant he could shed an additional overhead paying an accountant to check the books before the tax assessment was submitted. To Victor, it felt like there was a lot of unnecessary and unwelcome drama in his life. He ought to be going home to his wife and two small children, but instead he would have to clean the café now on top of the other jobs to which he needed to attend.

Feeling the weight of responsibility pressing down on him, Victor let his shoulders sag. 'Albert, I have to get this cleaned up. I still have tasks in the kitchen which I didn't get to finish because of the palaver this afternoon, I think I have someone fiddling the books here to hide money being stolen and April wants the world to believe the thief is Kate. Furthermore, with Kate accused of murder, the café's ownership has to be in question. How exactly is it that you think you can help me?'

Albert was sorry about the mess Rex had made; he could see it wasn't a five-minute job to clean up again. His apology wouldn't achieve anything though, so he said, 'I want to investigate what did happen to Joel Clement and make sure your sister goes free. That will give this place a new owner, won't it?'

'Yeah,' Victor conceded.

'You said someone is fiddling the books? Can I take a look?'

Mushy Peas

In the rain outside, a shadow moved. Francis was watching the front of the café, waiting for the man inside to come out. The rain had given them exactly what they wanted – empty streets. Eugene was around the back in case their target – Francis liked to think of his victims as targets because it sounded cooler - left by that door instead. They hadn't been afforded the time to study his routines to pick the perfect place to grab him. Much like Joel Clement, the earl sent them to get the person he wanted and gave them an unrealistic timeframe in which to complete the task.

However, upon arrival, they discovered the owner had died without revealing the real name of the person they should take. He said Maddie Hayes, but no such person worked at the café and never had according to the waitress they spoke with earlier. Eugene asked her who the best baker was, which was how they came to be waiting for Victor Harris now.

Despite the lack of preparation, it looked like they were in luck. They watched everyone else leave, both men finding a dark corner in which to wait and observe. The outline plan had been to follow him home because the small amount of research they did get time for revealed he lived just a quarter mile from the café. They guessed he would walk, not drive, though they were yet to determine if their assumptions were accurate.

Regardless, before they could find out, the old man from earlier appeared with his dog and now he was inside with their target. Worse yet, it didn't look like they were leaving any time soon.

Francis was just thinking about calling Eugene when his phone began to vibrate. He spoke a single word as the call connected. 'Go.' He and Eugene were both ex special forces and favoured brevity in their exchanges.

'Is something happening?' Eugene asked. 'The lights in the back rooms started to come back on. I think I can see an old man in there with him now.' Eugene was inappropriately dressed for night ops and for the weather. His jacket was going to ruin if it got much wetter and his expensive Italian loafers were soaked right through already. He couldn't moan about it because Francis would scoff at his need to dress smartly.

Francis replied, 'That's the old man he was talking to earlier. I remember the giant dog.'

'Any idea who he is?' asked Eugene.

Francis pulled a face at his phone. 'How on Earth would I know who it is? I watched them go through to the back rooms. If they are in an office, can you see what they are doing?'

Eugene grunted, 'Sitting in front of a computer. This feels like a bust.'

'He won't like that,' muttered Francis, referring to the earl's lack of patience.

'Tough,' growled Eugene as his stomach rumbled. 'We can't work miracles and I'm not rushing this and getting caught just because the earl wants it done fast. Besides, I'm getting hungry.'

'Fish 'n' chips?' suggested Francis thinking some dinner sounded like a good idea.

'You'd better call him and let him know,' Eugene insisted, quite certain he didn't want to be the one to break the news.

Francis curled his lip. 'Why me? Why don't you call him?'

'Because he likes you.'

'He doesn't even remember my name,' Francis protested.

Eugene chuckled. 'He doesn't remember anyone's name. You call him and I'll buy dinner.'

Francis took a second to weigh up the proposed bargain. 'All right, but I want mushy peas too.'

Dodgy Accounting

In the back office of the Clanger Café, Albert sat in front of the computer while Victor leaned over him to navigate to the accounts.

'Kate switched the firm across to a software platform that she said was easier to follow and would do a lot of the work for us. It caused untold drama with April because she's been here since before computers existed. I don't know when the previous owners shifted her onto a computer, but she was using a spreadsheet she'd created herself. I don't think anyone else could hope to understand it which she thought made her irreplaceable. It really put her nose out of joint when Joel announced Kate was taking over the bookkeeping and she made so much noise about her rights being unfairly undermined that Joel relented and had Kate show April how the system worked.'

'That's how she came to take over today the moment Kate was taken away and how she would know if someone were fiddling the books,' Albert concluded.

Victor nodded as he pulled up a second chair to sit next to the old man. 'That's right.'

Questions were forming a queue in his head already, but Albert asked the most obvious one, 'If Kate is the accountant, how come she was working behind the counter and cleaning away plates?'

Victor flipped his eyebrows. 'This is a small, family business, everyone switches between tasks and mucks in to help out. In fact, most of the people working here are related. Even April – one of our youngest, Shannon, is her sister's granddaughter.'

Albert pursed his lips and looked at the screen. 'Have you spotted any accounting anomalies that might make you believe April is right?'

'Me?' Victor flared his eyes. 'Goodness, no. I have no idea what all those lines of numbers mean. I'm just a guy that is good with pastry. Shall I leave you with it? I need to start cleaning up.'

Albert's reply came without him needing to think. 'Sure.' His attention was already on the screen. A murder, possible embezzlement: he wouldn't have to worry about finding his book boring or the people in the pub rowdy.' He heard Victor ask something about a cup of tea and couldn't say afterwards, what answer he might have given - the pull of the mystery was too great.

Rex sniffed around the office. It was a small space, roughly ten feet by ten feet with filing cabinets along one wall and shelves covered in box folders along another. He wanted to shake his fur properly, but when he lined himself up to do so, his human placed a hand on his head and begged that he lie down. He complied with a loud harrumph, making his feelings clear.

Above him, his human silently scanned along the rows of numbers.

Disappointment

'Why are you not on the return leg?' he demanded to know.

Francis sighed and bit his lip. He'd worked for worse employers, far worse now that he gave it some thought, but the earl had never worked a day in his life. He didn't clean, he didn't cook, he didn't lift a finger unless it was to pluck a morsel of food from a dish. He had no concept of what doing anything took with regard to effort, investment of time, and to a greater or lesser degree, depending on the task, luck. He simply expected things to happen because he wanted it to be done.

'We have been unable, at this time, to acquire the target,' Francis attempted to explain.

'Acquire the target?' repeated Earl Bacon, the words dripping from his mouth as if something unpleasant had found its way in there. 'That sounds like an excuse to me. I don't like excuses. I want that chef brought here and I want you to make sure you have the right one this time. I don't like being disappointed and you are disappointing me.' He already knew that Maddie Hayes was a made-up name and had recovered from the shock. That Joel Clement would lie to him was unfathomable, and he hated that he was now relying on his two muscular idiots to bring him the person they claimed was the one he truly wanted.

Francis exhaled slowly through his nose and fantasised about squeezing his employer's neck. The only good thing about his employer was that he was predictable. Well, that and he paid well. The earl had so much money it no longer had any meaning to him. He was utterly bonkers with all his talk of the world ending. He planned to live in an underground bunker and gorge himself to death on the world's finest food. He could buy whatever he wanted, but many of the things on his list of required foods were not the sort of thing a person could easily buy in bulk quantities. Also, getting them to his bunker, which he wanted as few people as possible to know the location of, meant secretive movements and that was why he employed Eugene and Francis. They were to arrange to obtain certain commodities, and people. The earl had a list of people he wanted to work in his kitchen. They were captives, of course, not employees, but the earl was crazy enough to believe he was saving them. On top of cooks and chefs and such, there were people to look after livestock, farmers to grow his plants, which was a highly specialised thing because it was all underground. He had three men just for mushrooms!

The saved, as the earl liked to call them, were all prisoners, but they were well-treated provided they accepted escape was impossible. Poor Joel Clement was the first person they'd had to kill for their new employer, but not the first person either man had killed. The list was well into double figures for each of them. Some were legitimate kills from their days in the special forces, but there had been an equal number since.

Francis quickly snaffled a chip from his bag before responding to his boss. 'We are waiting for an opportunity to take the target cleanly, Your Earlness. I anticipate this will occur very soon, certainly in the next twenty-four hours.'

'You had just better make sure it does,' snapped the earl. He knew how to handle men like Francis. He could trace his family's lineage all the way back to King Henry the seventh's court. His family had been lording it over lesser men for centuries. The general populace were layabouts and brigands the lot of them and could only be controlled with a firm hand.

Eugene and Francis had decided they quite fancied a couple of pints and an early night. The earl had them working all kinds of hours, but away from his constant demands they could claim it took longer than expected to safely obtain Victor Harris and who could possibly prove otherwise? They would come back in the morning and maybe intercept him on his way to work.

Stuffing another vinegar-soaked chip into his mouth, Francis repeated his promise to return within twenty-four hours and ended the call.

Bookkeeping

Albert was no accountant, but he knew his way around a set of books. It was one of the things he'd taught himself as part of his job. He wanted to know as much as he could and believed his determination to have a rounded education was what helped him rise through the ranks of the Kent Police while others floundered. Money was so often the motivation behind the murders he investigated, that having a basic knowledge of cashflow, profit and loss, and other regular accounting statements helped him zero in on what might be going on.

Not so this time.

If there were false entries here, or numbers that failed to tally, he wasn't seeing them. Checking over his shoulder to listen for Victor, he reached into his jacket to produce his phone.

'Hi, dad?' said his daughter, Selina, when she answered.

Albert tried to split his phone calls between his children, wanting to limit the number of times he asked them to do things for him so he wouldn't seem like he was always snooping into someone's business. Of course, he knew his kids talked to each other, so his attempts at subterfuge were largely pointless, but he did it anyway.

'Hello, Selina, how are you and how are my grandchildren?' he asked to get the conversation started.

'Everyone is sick, actually. Except me, that is. Some kind of tummy bug. The kids started exploding from both ends this morning and now their father is too. I've had to take the day off to deal with them all.'

This was not the news Albert wanted to hear. Obviously, he never wanted to hear that his grandchildren were ill, but he wanted Selina to be in work and able to use her contacts to get the books checked over. At home, and with a sick family, she wasn't in a position to help and he wouldn't ask.

'That's terrible,' he said, secretly wishing he'd called Randall now because he didn't have children or a wife. 'Do you feel okay?'

Selina sighed. 'I could do without this, but yes, I'm fine. I don't get sick.'

Albert remembered how rare it was for her to ever be ill as a child. 'No. No, you don't, do you? Well, I guess I had better let you get back to it then. Sounds like you have your hands full.'

'No, Dad,' Selina protested. 'I could do with a break from them. You called me so you must have time to chat. Where are you tonight? Still in Biggleswade?' His daughter wanted to chat and he could hardly push her away to call one of his other children who might be able to help instead, but as he regaled her with how his clanger class had gone and how tasty the treat had been, he spotted a line on the screen that didn't tally. He'd needed longer to scrutinise the accounts, that was all. Now that he'd seen the first one, he saw a second too. They were small numbers, not on the main profit and loss statement, but on the daily takings tallies. He certainly wouldn't have spotted them if he hadn't been looking, but April had.

They were small numbers, twenty pounds one day, ten pounds on another but not two days in a row. He continued to look back at the sheets. Each monthly tally showed a set of figures that matched, and the monthly profit and loss statement hid the missing money, but the daily tallies, where the goods sold ought to match the money taken for them, had holes in. One could put them down to the person on the till

41

accidentally handing over the wrong change, but there were too many instances for that, and it was all exact numbers.

Now that he'd identified what looked like petty theft - someone taking notes from the till - Albert had to consider what it meant and if it had anything to do with Joel Clement's murder.

'Dad!'

Snapped back to reality, Albert realised Selina had been talking and probably asking him questions, but he hadn't spoken in over a minute. 'Sorry, sweetheart, I zoned out there for a moment, didn't I? I should probably get an early night. All the excitement recently has left me feeling tired.' He faked a yawn, making it audible as part of his act.

Selina sounded a little worried when she replied, 'Are you sure you're all right, Dad? You can come home any time you want. I will come and get you. Or one of the boys will. It's no bother.'

They were still trying to get him to cancel or cut short his trip. They all worried for no good reason. It made him want to fast forward their lives so they could be nearly eighty too. Maybe then they would see that scoring a few years didn't make a person decrepit.

'I'm fine, sweetheart,' he assured her, believing wholeheartedly that it was true. 'I'm having fun and so is Rex. You've nothing to worry about.'

'Dad, you keep getting mixed up in murder cases. Randall got hurt in Bakewell and I had to come there with Gary to help you out.'

Albert chuckled, 'Yeah. That was a lot of fun, wasn't it?'

'No, Dad. It was dangerous. You could have been hurt. Randall *was* hurt.'

'It all ended well enough,' Albert grumbled, beginning to feel a little put upon.

Relenting, Selina said, 'Okay, Dad. Look I've got to go. I can hear one of the kids moving about upstairs which probably means they are about to throw up again. Just take care of yourself, okay?'

'Of course, love.' The call ended, but he'd been looking at the lines of numbers the whole time and there was no doubt someone had been taking money.

He pulled open the drawer in the desk to see if there was anything in it of interest. A notebook with some annotations would be nice, he thought as he leafed through the clutter. Perhaps he needed to speak with April. She didn't portray herself as someone a person might wish to interview, but she clearly thought she knew something, and he needed to know what it was.

Victor reappeared in the doorway. He was perspiring slightly from the effort of getting the café cleaned to an acceptable standard as swiftly as possible. 'Find anything?' he asked.

Albert took a few moments to point out the small discrepancies, indicating each line and figure with a finger and then hypothesising about the notes being taken from the till as one way in which the money might have gone missing.

Victor skewed his face to the side in thought. 'Kate would have noticed that, wouldn't she?' he asked it as a question, but Albert thought the man already knew the answer.

'They would have stood out,' he replied quietly. 'Any accountant would have seen them.'

Victor was shaking his head, accepting what he could see but refusing to believe it anyway. 'There's no way Kate was stealing from the business. No way. Just like there's no way she killed Joel.'

'Well then. I guess we should ask her about it.'

'We can do that?' asked Victor. 'I didn't think they would let me near her.'

Albert tipped his chair back. 'At the station? No, they won't. Not without very good reason. They will let her make a phone call though. We just have to get a message to her, so she calls us.' In his head, Albert was thinking about his two sons and wondering which he could use to get a message to Kate Harris. He had a short list of questions he wanted answers to and the only way to get them, unless DS Craig felt like sharing, which he highly doubted, was to have Randall or Gary go through a back door.

'Can we do that now?' asked Victor.

Albert glanced at the clock on the computer and shook his head. 'Unlikely, I will need to set that up.' In truth, Victor could go to the station and have a message to call him passed on. They would probably do it, but Albert wanted to be involved and this way was more likely to yield a result.

Hanging his head, Victor released a breath as if he'd been holding it. 'Poor Kate.' At the sound of his human's name, Hans looked up, making eye contact with Victor. 'And what am I going to do with you?' he asked the dog.

Hans tilted his head to the side, wondering what he was being asked.

Rex saw a great opportunity to get his own back for some of the snarky dog's comments, but rubbing in that his human was gone and might not come back was too cruel for him to consider, so he moved to get to his own human for a head rub and accidentally on purpose knocked the dachshund over as he barged past.

'Hey, watch it!' growled Hans.

'You can't take him home with you?' enquired Albert, thinking that to be the obvious solution.

Victor rubbed his chin. 'I'm not sure how that would be received; my wife is not a fan of dogs in general and the kids will get overexcited and then want one of their own.' Scratching his chin, he concluded. 'I guess it will be okay for a few nights. Do you think he is housebroken?'

'Housebroken!' exclaimed Hans, righteous indignation making him want to bite the human's ankle.

Rex sniggered, which just made things worse.

'I suppose it's a bit late to be coming up with another plan,' Victor sighed. At his feet, the two dogs were growling at each other.

'Your mother likes to hang out with three-legged dogs at the docks,' snarled Hans.

'Your mother drives a motorised doggie wheelchair!' snapped Rex. 'She's not crippled, she just likes that she can go to the park and reverse it around to all the dogs one at a time.'

Hans couldn't believe his ears. 'Oh, yeah? Well your mother likes to do it standing up like a human!'

Rex snorted; he was so much better at this than the dachshund. It came from his time in uniform. You hang around with a bunch of other dogs in tough jobs and you get used to throwing banter around. Cruelly, he lowered his head to deliver his next line. 'So does your father.'

Hans went mental, his little feet scrabbling across the tile as he flung himself at Rex. One twentieth of the size, he was still going to try to kill the enormous German Shepherd, even if he had to choke the dog to death by getting stuck in his throat.

Victor saw Hans lunge forward, his teeth snapping. 'Whoa!'

'I don't think they are playing,' said Albert as Victor snatched the dachshund from the floor just before he threw himself into Rex's mouth.

Hans continued to throw insults as Victor held him off the floor with two hands. 'It's time I was getting home. Are you going to be in town for long?'

Albert pushed back against his chair, converting the motion to get onto his old, tired legs. 'One of the joys of being old and retired, is that a person can choose to do whatever they want and even change their mind halfway through. I shall stay here until I choose to move on. I cannot promise to unearth Joel's killer but, if I can, I will find enough evidence to get your sister released.' Albert was taking the sensible approach and not promising anything he didn't know for certain he could deliver, but the recent week and a half of travelling the country had reignited a passion for investigating that had been hidden for many years. When he retired, Petunia had all manner of activities to keep him busy: gardening, sorting out the attic, days out to visit relatives or to just go to a tearoom. When he lost her, he was truly lost for a while. Adrift with no shore in sight and no anchor to tether him, it was a chance encounter that led him back to feeling that he had something akin to a purpose and had he not found it,

46

he wondered if perhaps he might have just faded away to nothing. Poking his nose into what might be happening at the Clanger Café was no chore at all. It was a gift.

'Why are you helping?' asked Victor. 'I mean, don't get me wrong, I'm grateful, but what's in it for you? You don't know us.'

Albert didn't want to give the long-winded explanation, so he just said, 'It gives me purpose.'

Revelations

It was the kind of mission one is born into, or perhaps one that a dog finds thrust upon them, but whatever the case, Rex knew it was his solemn destiny to fight against the fluffy-tailed menace until his last breath was expended.

His human didn't seem to understand the threat they posed, often shouting for him to leave them alone, but Rex knew. Rex knew they would take over the garden and the house if he wasn't there to keep them at bay.

Something had changed recently though. They seemed more organised, more … coordinated. Rex shuddered and looked at the tree again. He liked the tree. There were only three trees in his human's garden and the sycamore was his favourite – he needed to pee somewhere. However, now that he had finished and wanted to return to the house where his human was watching the flat thing on the wall with the pictures and sounds but no smell, Rex found he was facing a platoon of squirrels.

He barked a warning at them, which ought to have sent them scattering, their tiny limbs seeming to defy gravity as they whizzed across the lawn to disappear up a tree or over the fences on either side. Not this time though; they stood their ground, and it was unnerving. He barked again, louder this time and with some extra bass in his voice. Normally, he would have charged at them the moment he saw them on the ground, but their confidence was making him hesitate.

Telling himself today was the day he would catch one and finally be able to show them what they could expect if they came into his territory, he almost backed away when one of them stepped forward. They were all up on their hind legs, their tails twitching occasionally, but the one who advanced lifted one little forelimb, made a fist, and drove it down to smack into the palm of his other paw.

What was going on? Did he charge them or not? Why were they acting like they could win this fight? There were lots of them, but not enough to do a dog his size any damage. If they bit him, would he even notice?

Before he could reach a decision, another stepped forward, this one driving a tiny fist up into the air as it screeched a battle cry. Rex felt his legs twitch. Suddenly, he wanted to run away.

'Daft dog,' muttered Albert as he swung his legs out of bed. 'Whatever are you dreaming about to be twitching like that? It looks like you are running away from a monster.' Twisting and tilting his neck and rolling his shoulders, Albert got himself ready to get to his feet. Rex's paws were twitching like crazy as the dog's jowls spasmed with excited high-pitched barks. Whatever dream he was having looked like it involved running.

Albert slept soundly after opting to stop in the bar, when he finally made it through the rain, for a swift gin and tonic that turned into two. He got a packet of crisps each for him and the dog and idled away nearly an hour pondering the Kate Harris case. There wasn't much to go on. There certainly wasn't much in Kate's favour yet, which was something he needed to try to correct today. His conversation with Randall had gone better than the one with Selina. It had been more productive certainly, and he knew a little more about the Joel Clement murder now. Rounding off the conversation, Randall promised to get a message to Kate Harris – something he could do with a phone call – and bade his father goodnight with a promise to email more information overnight.

With all that in mind and possessing the singular goal of proving Kate Harris's innocence, Albert determined he would start in earnest after breakfast. First, he needed the bathroom and Rex would need a walk.

Like the three previous stops on his tour around the country, Biggleswade was abundant with green spaces. Where he lived in Kent was too, the small village of East Malling sitting amid lush farmland, orchards, vineyards, and open countryside. In Kent, he knew he wouldn't have to go far to find himself in an urban sprawl of concrete and high-rise buildings, or in a purpose-built commercial district of firms. Here though, he didn't think there was anything like that for miles and when a more populated area was found, it wasn't like at home, where the houses were stacked on top of one another for mile after mile, it was ancient and beautiful towns and cities with interesting architecture.

Walking Rex through Biggleswade now, he marvelled at how many of the buildings appeared to have stood for more than a century. There were leaflets for local attractions in the reception of the pub. Leafing through the rack last night, he'd found one which provided a written guided dog walk that would take in the nearby river. The drizzle of the previous evening was gone, the skies clear again so, time permitting, he wanted to test his endurance with a longer walk before he left. For now though, he planned to let the dog do what he needed and get back for breakfast.

Rex had his head down, sniffing his way along the pavement and stopping periodically to mark his scent. However, he stopped when they reached a crossroad because a very familiar scent assailed his nostrils – it was the annoying dachshund!

Albert saw Rex stiffen. 'What is it, boy?'

With his head lifted and turned to the wind, Rex snuffled in a deep pocket of air. He was right about the dachshund but there was something else he recognised there too. He tried again, but the scent proved elusive. When he reopened his eyes – he always shut them to heighten his sense of smell – he could see Hans coming toward him.

50

Albert grinned and waved. He'd taken Victor's number the previous evening before they went their separate ways but hadn't asked the man where he lived. Since he was out walking the dachshund this morning, it had to be somewhere close.

Rex kept his mouth shut and waited for Hans to come to him. The small dog was powering forward, doing his best to drag his human along in his need to close the distance. Would he pick up with the insults and bad attitude from last night? Or would a little sleep have mellowed him?

'Hey, wolf. Yo momma smells like a lamppost and she likes it.'

Sleep didn't help then, sighed Rex to himself, looking at his human. 'Do we have to hang out with the dachshund? He's a little annoying.'

Albert, aware that his dog was able to smell things he couldn't, had begun to wonder over the last week if Rex might actually be trying to draw his attention to things he was missing. The dog had a habit of looking right at him and making noises; sort of a combination of barking, whining and an odd chuffing noise. He looked down at him now with a frown. 'Are you trying to tell me something, Rex?' he asked, perplexed that the dog might be that clever while simultaneously annoyed that he couldn't understand it if he was. 'What is it?'

'The dachshund is an annoying, mouthy little butt weasel. I'd rather hang out with a cat,' explained Rex, saying it slowly so his human might understand.

'The dachshund?' asked Albert, guessing that might be what had his dog all excited.

Rex couldn't believe it! His human was not only paying enough attention to know Rex was telling him something, he was even starting to understand. He spun on the spot with excitement and wagged his tail.

'You're super excited to see Hans again because we never spend any time with dogs?'

Rex hung his head.

'Morning, Albert,' hallooed Victor, crossing the street to get to them.

'Good morning, Victor and Hans. Rex is ever so pleased to see Hans again. I think they must have hit it off last night.

Rex said something rude.

'Just taking him for a walk?' Victor asked conversationally.

'Yes. He is used to getting some exercise between his breakfast and mine.'

'I'm just on my way to the station to see if I can't speak with Kate or get a message to her.'

'Oh, ah, hold on a moment.' Victor's announcement reminded Albert to check his phone for messages. Randall promised to do what he could last night, which might mean the information Albert wanted was already in an email waiting to be read. That Victor hadn't already had a call from her might mean the message was yet to be passed, or wasn't going to be passed, or even that Kate didn't want to speak with anyone.

Albert got his phone out but a swift patting down of his pockets revealed his reading glasses were back at the pub on his nightstand. 'I don't have my reading glasses,' he explained, holding the phone out for Victor to see the screen. 'Can you see an email from Randall?'

Victor scrutinised the list of emails, spotting one with randallsmith in the email address third from the top. 'Yes. Do you want me to read it?'

'Yes, please.'

Victor took the offered phone so he could operate it and read the email aloud.

'Dad, I do hope you are not poking your nose in again. I read about that business in Stilton, you know. The murder victim you asked about was garrotted with a piece of rope. As you know, this throws ambiguity on the gender of the killer.'

Victor looked up from the phone. 'What does he mean by ambiguity?'

'Statistically, some methods of murder are favoured by one gender or the other. It's not a hard rule and would never be used to argue a case, but if it were strangulation, the case is that many women do not have the strength to overpower a man and hold a choke on for long enough. A woman could easily use a garrotte though, coming from behind to cut off air to the lungs and blood to the brain.'

'Right.' It was all Victor could think of to say in response to the clinical explanation. He brought his eyes back to the screen.

'The victim was found outside of a village called Llandinam in Wales.'

Victor tore his eyes from the screen again. 'Wales? What on Earth was Joel doing in Wales?'

Albert of course had no idea, but it was an intriguing question. The man had gone to a pub on his way home and was found dead the following day a hundred and something miles away in a different country. That the information surprised Victor also meant his sister had chosen to not share what she knew with him.

'Does he have any family that way who he might want to visit?' Albert hazarded a guess.

Victor didn't know. 'I don't think so, but I would have to check to be sure.' Once again, he went back to the screen.

'The coroner's report listed post-mortem injuries congruent with having been thrown from a moving car - it looks like the killers just dropped him at the side of the road without slowing down. There's not a lot else to tell you other than they have a woman in custody. She has motive and opportunity. She also has a record. If I were a betting man, I'd say they had the right person.'

Victor's voice trailed off as he finished reading, the final line the absolute opposite of what he wanted to hear, and he could feel Albert's gaze boring into the side of his head.

'What is her record for?' Albert enquired, wishing he'd thought to ask about her history a little sooner.

'GBH,' Victor replied quietly and glumly, using the standard abbreviation of Grievous Bodily Harm. As a former police officer, Albert knew that to be accused or convicted of GBH, a person had to cause sufficient harm to a person to permanently disfigure them or break bones. A single drop of blood that falls outside of the body can be classed as GBH and a weapon does not need to be used, only the intent to do harm has to be proven. 'She was ...' he was about to say she was innocent, but that wasn't strictly true. 'It was an accident. She didn't mean to hurt the other girl.'

'Tell me,' sighed Albert, wondering if he ought to drop the whole thing and head to York early.

'It was her eighteenth birthday. There's not a lot around here for the youngsters to get excited about so she headed into Cambridge with a bunch of her friends. They had drinks and went to a club and such. Then she got into a fight. It would have been nothing, just a bad memory at the

54

end of a good night out, but they were on some stairs and the girl fell. The police came and the other girl's friends all said Kate shoved her. I don't know if she did or not. Kate always denied it, but she went to jail for three months anyway and will always have a record. That's not going to help her, is it?'

Albert pursed his lips. 'No. It will not.' Homewrecker, fiddling the books, criminal record for violent assault, and now accused of murder. Was he on a fool's errand or not? He'd seen her eyes when they came to arrest her and that was all he was using to justify his desire to help. Could she be clever enough to fake what looked like a natural reaction?

Three feet below the humans' conversation, Rex was ignoring the dachshund's taunts, busying himself with sniffing the air instead when a scent made his eyes pop open. It was there again, the blended scent of the two men from the café. They were in the café yesterday afternoon, then at least one of them was outside the café when he and his human went back in the evening, and now he could smell them both here. It was faint, coming on the breeze. He got to his feet and turned into the wind. The air wasn't moving much, just a faint whisper of it drifting along, and it carried all manner of different scents.

'Hey, wolf,' Hans was trying to get through Rex's thick skin and beginning to get upset that the dog could continue to ignore him.

Rex glanced down. 'Can you smell that?'

'Smell what?' Was this a trick where the stupid lump of a German Shepherd was going to lure him into smelling a fart? 'I can smell everything. You'll have to be more specific.'

Rex turned his face back into the wind, but he kept his eyes open as he searched for the source. 'There were two men in the café yesterday,' Rex explained. 'They are here again now.'

'Yeah. What about it? They were in my human's house as well. They left their stink all over it.'

Rex whipped his head around so fast the dachshund took a step back in surprise. 'They were in your house and you didn't think to mention it? You live with two humans, right? You know something bad happened to one of them and the other one is being blamed for it.'

Hans could do nothing but stare at the larger dog in mute shock. 'What do you mean something happened to him? How do you know that?'

'Because I listen to the humans.' Rex found this with a lot of dogs. They had one favourite human they would generally pay some attention to but for the most part, humans babbled a lot of gibberish and it wasn't worth listening to. Dogs learned at an early age that they should just stop paying attention. That was what Hans had done. 'Your human, the female one?'

'The bitch?'

'Yes, humans don't like that word. I have no idea why, but they don't, so we'll call her the female human.'

'Okay.'

'Well, my human is trying to work out what happened to your other human, and if he doesn't, you might not get to see your female human again. Do you get it now?'

Hans sniffed the air. 'And you think the two humans from the café might have something to do with it?'

'If they were in your house, I do.'

Hans thought about that. 'But people come to the house all the time. My humans are always inviting other humans in. It's one of the best things

56

about living with humans; there is always someone new to make a fuss of you.'

Rex would have rolled his eyes if he knew how to. The dachshund was right about the humans, of course, just not in this case. 'You don't think it's at all suspicious that they are here now somewhere?'

Hans didn't have an answer, but he didn't like being talked down to or made to feel like he was inadequate. He had enough self-doubt because his size and shape placed him on the low end of the scale when it came to speed, strength, fighting ability, and a dozen other attributes he wanted to be better at. Overall, it gave him a complex which he fought hard against and would happily turn to aggression as a first port of call when challenged.

Rex saw that the dachshund was getting angry again and chose to ignore him. 'We're being followed,' he told Albert, barking the news loudly enough to get his human's attention.

His conversation interrupted; Albert looked down at Rex. 'What is it, boy? Do you need to find a spot to go? I should move on,' he told Victor.

A Cunning Plan

'Who is that old guy with the dog?' The question was muttered by Eugene, who was already upset because he'd snagged his jacket on an overhanging bramble and now had a small tear in its right shoulder.

Francis wanted to know as well. They looked into Victor Harris last night, taking time to do some research the way they should have before they set off. The point is, they knew his father had died two years ago, so whoever the old man was, he wasn't a relative. He was in the way though. The earl might have given them a day's grace to get the job done, but he would blow his top if they didn't report that they had his chef in their van the next time they called.

Francis chose to be stoical. 'Look, we always knew grabbing him in daylight on his way to work was a long shot.'

'He's not on his way to work though. The café is in the other direction. He's just out walking his dog. We don't even need to follow him. We can go back to his house with the van and wait for him to walk by. You casually step out in front of him and ask him the time. I'll open the side door and hit him with the stun gun, then we both dump him into the van and scarper. How does that sound?'

Francis ran the images through his head and had to admit his partner's plan had many merits. 'It's certainly worth a shot,' he conceded.

'That's why I'm the brains of this outfit,' Eugene boasted.

'You're certainly not the muscle,' muttered Francis just loud enough for Eugene to hear.

'What? What was that? Are you suggesting that you are stronger than me?' Eugene was outraged by the suggestion even though he secretly worried it might be true.

Francis didn't respond for a moment. Something about the big dog was troubling him. They were watching them move away now; the old man and the target were walking side by side and chatting as if they were old friends.

Huffing out a breath, Francis said, 'Let's get back to the van.' He didn't wait for Eugene to respond; he was already heading back the way they had come. They'd been watching Victor Harris walk his dog and were getting ready to pounce when the old man appeared. But it was just too dodgy to snatch their target with someone else around. They could just eliminate him, but the dog would make noise and that might attract other people to look their way. It just wasn't worth the risk. There was something about that dog too. The big one, not the funny little sausage dog. The big one had looked right into the shadow where he stood out of sight last night, and then again this morning. Francis was certain neither he nor Eugene could be seen but the dog had been staring directly at them.

If it came to it, he would kill the dog and the old man. They had to make their move today, but with luck, Eugene would be right about them being able to snatch Harris from the side of the road as he came back to his house. Unfortunately, in the meantime, he had to listen to Eugene spouting on about how they were going to have a bench press contest when they got back to the gym.

Choosing to delay breakfast, despite the faint rumble in his stomach, Albert said, 'I'll walk with you.'

'You're coming to the station?' Victor sounded surprised. 'I thought you were heading back to your hotel for breakfast.'

'I'll get there,' Albert assured him. 'You read the last part of my son's message. He spoke with the duty sergeant last night so the request for Kate to call you has either been passed because she will have been woken by now, assuming she got any sleep, or it will not be passed at all. My guess is that the station isn't far away.' The guess was based on the size of Biggleswade. It was several times larger than Stilton, the last place he and Rex had stayed, but still small enough that a person could walk from one end to the other in a matter of minutes.

'It's on the other side of town,' he replied, by which Albert assumed Victor meant on the other side of the busy B road which bisected the town into two halves. 'It should take about five minutes to get to from here.'

Listening to his stomach gurgle, Albert felt thankful the delay to his full English platter wouldn't be a long one. Going to the police station might very well prove fruitless, but it would give them a chance to ask a few questions about Kate. Replaying Randall's email in his head, his son made it sound like the conviction was already assured. If the police in Biggleswade believed that, they wouldn't spend time interviewing her, they would have taken her statement yesterday, confirmed she had no alibi, and probably had her scheduled for transfer to prison this morning.

Albert didn't feel sorry for her; he learned to detach himself from such unhelpful emotions a long time ago, and his investigation had switched from attempting to prove she was innocent, to determining for himself if she was guilty or not. That might seem like a subtle change, but it was significant, nevertheless. The evidence pointed her way.

Though the air was cool, it was a pleasant walk and they passed people who were most likely on their way to work, hurrying here and there in their cars or on foot. Supermarkets were open, so too small cafés selling breakfast and businesses like bakeries, the smell of fresh bread filling Albert's nostrils in a tempting manner.

Rex caught a whiff on the wind, sucking in a deep noseful of air to confirm what his first sniff told him. His own stomach rumbled, and he groaned with excitement, 'Oh, yeah!'

Hans glanced at him, the two dogs locking eyes for a moment as they both savoured the dominant smell. 'Kebab!' they squealed in tandem and both dogs surged forward. Straining against their collars to find the source of the smell which seemed to fill the air and push out everything else. Their reaction caught the humans off guard.

'Crickey!' Albert stumbled slightly as Rex tugged his right arm forward.

Victor too, though steadier on his feet, found Hans was suddenly trying to run where a moment ago he was content to walk. 'What's got into them?' he asked.

The smell was getting stronger, Rex's nose leading him on, but he missed a stray piece of meat at the side of the road which Hans fell upon with glee.

'Did you see what that was?' asked Victor. He'd never had a dog, and thus wasn't used to dog behaviour. Albert was though, and he'd danced to this tune before.

Scanning the pavement ahead, he spotted the abandoned kebab. It was a sad truth that late-night kebab shops were the refuge of public house evictees, where a pitta bread full of meat acted as a compass to steer the inebriated home. Held in both hands like a divining rod, the meaty grease-laden receptacle of bread all too often ended up either partially, or completely on the ground where it remained until someone cleared it away. Albert had tried one once and hadn't enjoyed it. Though he suspected what he'd tasted was a poor imitation of a nation's cuisine, he had never tried one since.

Rex, however, homed in on an abandoned kebab like a bee to honey.

Rex could see it now, his powerful nose getting him close enough that he no longer needed it, but as Rex began to celebrate the feast to come, his collar began to tug in a different direction. His human wanted to cross the road!

He dug his claws into the pavement, searching for purchase mere feet from his prize.

'Come along, Rex,' Albert insisted. 'You are not eating a mouldy old kebab that's been out in the rain!' Beside him, Victor was having the same drama with Hans but on a far more manageable scale. The wiener was likewise digging his claws in and trying to get his body to the scattered remains of someone's supper, but Victor looped a hand under his belly, hoisting him into the air to defeat his attempts to snag another piece of meat.

Crossing the road, it was a good thing Albert couldn't translate what Rex said because none of it was printable.

At the station, they were met by a sergeant on the front desk. It was a small police station, barely big enough to hold a detainee though Albert was sure they would have several small cells tucked away behind the scenes. The sergeant was clean shaven and well into his forties, grey specks winning the battle against his dark brown hair, and he had a small scar by his left ear which might have a story behind it. It had puckered marks on either side where the skin had been sewn back together, and though clearly many years old, the white scar tissue stood in contrast to the rest of his lightly tanned skin.

'Good morning, gentlemen?' he gave them his professional face, waiting to hear what malady they might have to report.

On their way in, Albert had requested that Victor let him speak, his experience in handling the police likely to prove to their advantage.

'Good morning,' Albert replied. Taking a second to instruct Rex to sit, he came right up to the counter. 'You have a suspect in custody, her name is Kate Harris. I am hoping to be able to speak with her, either directly, or via a telephone.'

Opting to answer a question that hadn't been asked, the sergeant said, 'She is due to be transferred to HMP Bedford shortly.'

Albert warned Victor this was likely to be the case but felt the man tense up at the news anyway. 'This is her brother,' Albert explained. 'And her dog,' he indicated Hans. He knew there was no sense in stating that the police had the wrong person. He had no proof to back up such a claim, he wasn't entirely certain they did have the wrong person, and doing so *always* upset the officers in question. Always. 'Her arrest was a surprise to her family and coworkers; she holds a position of responsibility at the Clanger café and her unexpected absence may impact the firm negatively. For the sake of other people, innocent of any crime, having her answer a few questions would prevent loss of business. I'm sure you, as a Bedfordshire man, would hate to see the Clanger Café close.' Albert's carefully worded request hadn't contained a single question, just the suggestion of negative impact on the community the sergeant undoubtedly held dear. Watching the man's face, he knew he'd hit home and delivered the winning line. 'Just a few words over the phone, Sergeant, that's all. May we, please?'

Now he was stuck. The sergeant's easiest course of action was to do nothing and have no one speak to the suspect. She would be out of his hair shortly and someone else's problem. He had no legal reason to let the old man see or speak to Kate Harris, but what if the Clanger Café closed? He did like a clanger when the mood took him. What harm could a few words over the phone do?

'Okay. But I must limit you to five minutes. There is no easy way to arrange a phone call so I will have a constable escort one of you back to the cells. You can talk through the door. Good enough?'

Albert inclined his head. 'Thank you, Sergeant. We will wait here until you are ready for us.'

What Albert didn't know was that the station in Biggleswade was due to be closed in less than a month. It was too expensive to keep on: budget cuts, manning shortages, and lack of crime in the community, all demanded the resources be reallocated elsewhere. Biggleswade would be covered from the larger hub in Bedford. That was why there was no phone; much of the building's infrastructure had already been reclaimed.

'You should go,' suggested Victor. 'I want to see her, but you are the one with the questions.'

Albert opened his mouth to argue but closed it again because Victor was right. Victor could ask the questions, but if anything needed to be clarified or another question occurred, he wouldn't be in a position to recognise what needed to be done.

They were made to wait only ten minutes before a young constable appeared. A female officer, she was in her thirties and tall for a woman at close to six feet. Albert wondered about her heritage, questioning in his head whether her parents might be Hungarian or from one of the Slavic states. He kept quiet as she led him through to the rear of the small station, Rex getting left behind with Victor and Hans.

Behind the brightly painted and welcoming reception area, all the walls were painted with a light grey paint as if it were the inside of a battleship. Albert had never thought about it much when he was a serving officer, but looking at it now, the surroundings were a little depressing. Along a narrow corridor and around a bend, they reached a solid door with a metal grill at eye height. Through it, Albert could see another narrow corridor, this one had a blank wall on the left and four cell doors on the right. The doors were evenly spaced, the cells designed to be uniformly boring, but safe.

The constable paused at the outer door. 'Wait here, sir. I will bring Miss Harris from her cell and you can speak to her through this grate. Please, do not attempt to move around the station or leave this spot. When the prisoner approaches the door, do not attempt to pass her anything. Do not attempt to put your hand, or any other part of your body through the grate.' The list of what to do and not to do went on for a while.

Albert promised that he would do as instructed and waited patiently for the woman he met briefly, and only yesterday, to be released from her cell. Her curious eyes turned toward the hole in the outer cell block door and showed surprise when she saw who it was.

'Stay behind the line,' the constable barked at the back of Kate's head, making her twitch with its sudden harshness in the echoey corridor.

Albert offered her a warm smile. 'Hello again. You are probably wondering why I am here. I came with your brother, but they would only permit one of us to come through here.' Kate's smile had looked forced when he first met her which he knew now was because of Joel's murder. There was no trace of a smile today.

'What is it that you want?' Kate asked.

'I didn't get the chance to introduce myself yesterday. My name is Albert Smith. I ...'

'Albert Smith,' repeated the constable, interrupting his flow as her eyebrows bunched together in a frown. 'There was an older gentleman involved in an incident in Stilton two days ago. I heard he uncovered a money counterfeiting ring run by a senior chief inspector.'

Albert nodded. This might be easier with a little context. 'That was me,' he admitted. 'However, the investigation was led by a very capable young constable.' He told them dismissively. 'I have not been afforded a great deal of time, Kate, so I will get to the point. You are accused of murder and the case against you is a strong one. It may be lacking in hard evidence but what there is, combined with your lack of defence, may be enough to secure a conviction.'

She nodded sadly and turned her head away as a tear slipped from her left eye. 'That's what they keep telling me. They want me to confess because it will reduce my sentence. But I didn't do it.'

Albert believed his years of experience gave him something akin to a sixth sense when trying to separate lies from truth and Kate was telling him the truth. Accepting that she hadn't murdered her lover, he moved on to another question. 'At the café there are discrepancies in the bookkeeping. Can you explain them?'

Kate's jaw dropped. 'How can you possibly know about that?'

The how was of no consequence, but he answered, 'I am working with your brother. He believes you are innocent of all charges. Where is the missing money, Kate?'

'Why do you want to know about that?' she asked, frowning now, and looking like she wanted to argue. 'That has nothing to do with why I am in here. I didn't take the money if that is what you are asking.'

She was snapping at him, her anger close to the surface because of her predicament. Albert didn't take it personally and didn't react to it. 'It will help me to have a clear picture of what is going on. If you didn't kill Joel, it means someone else did, and the police are not looking for the killer because they believe you are guilty. I can only help you if I have the full picture.'

He watched as she bit her lip, deep in thought. 'I can't tell you about the missing money. It has nothing to do with Joel.' Albert sighed loudly in his frustration, but she started speaking again before he could say anything. 'Please help me, Albert. I didn't do this. I didn't take the money and I didn't hurt Joel. I loved him.'

'He set you up as a partner in the business. You stood to become the sole owner in the event of his death. You stole him away from his wife and children.'

'No, I didn't,' she whispered meekly, her head and eyes cast down to the floor. He'd been pushing her to see how she reacted.

'Time's up,' said a voice from behind him. Kate's eye snapped up and Albert turned on the spot to find the sergeant from the front desk peering around the corner. 'The transport will be here soon. Put her back in her cell.'

Albert drew in a slow breath, holding it for a few seconds as he wondered what else he could possibly ask her. She refused to give him a straight answer about the money which felt like an admission of guilt even though she claimed she didn't take it. She made him believe that she wasn't Joel Clement's killer, but she had all the motive and zero alibi. When he looked back up, what he saw was Kate's back as she returned through the door of her cell.

He was beginning to wish he had chosen to take his clanger to go yesterday.

Eggs

Victor needed to get to work. He and another chef alternated with two other chefs for who was on earlies or lates. Rising early didn't bother him though he was sure it would if he did it every day. The Clanger Café only shut two days each year: Christmas and Easter Sunday, so quite often the four primary chefs had to cover shifts so someone could take a holiday. He had an early yesterday, which meant a later start this morning, but he was about to be late for his late start. Though he knew everyone, with the exception of April, would accept why, he still felt he had to be there to help ensure the operation ran smoothly.

He hung around to hear what Albert had to report, then had to hurry away with a promise to see Albert later.

Left to his own devices, Albert wandered back to the pub to get his breakfast. They stopped serving at ten o'clock and he was running the chance of missing out if he didn't get moving.

He made it with time to spare, taking Rex in with him to save time. 'Now listen, Rex,' he made the dog look at him while he delivered a warning/request. 'I would like to enjoy my breakfast in peace, okay? That means, no running across the room because you have spotted a crumb of toast. No flipping me off my chair because you've seen a squirrel outside the window, and no accidentally-on-purpose tripping the waiter when he brings me my food. I have ordered you some eggs which you will get if we make it to the end of my breakfast without incident. Is that a deal?'

Rex only heard the part about there being eggs for him. The rest of what his human said was just background noise. He wagged his tail and looked about for the person with plates of food. There were two other couples in the room, all of whom had finished eating and were either chatting or reading a newspaper.

The waiter arrived with the plates, a steady mist of steam rising from each as the man placed them on the table. 'This one is yours,' said Albert, tilting it slightly so Rex could see.

Rex was on his feet and poised to eat. Drool dripped from his lower jaw in anticipation of the four fried eggs he was about to inhale. Until his human took them away and placed them in the middle of the table, that is. 'You get them when I finish mine,' chided Albert.

Huffing with disappointment, Rex stared at the plate, focussing his thoughts, and concentrating hard. It refused to levitate. Irked at being outsmarted by his human, Rex harrumphed to the carpet and turned his back.

At the table, Albert was also drooling, though less visibly than his dog. His breakfast had two thick bacon chops, each of which were presented with a crispy, yet still glistening, layer of fat running around the outside. It was like having crackling for breakfast. Complimented by black pudding, sausages, fried eggs, meaty portabella mushrooms – oven baked and served whole – plus fried bread, beans, and grilled tomato. He kept telling himself to order the kippers for a change, but the tempting plates of evil breakfast goodness suckered him in every time. Besides, Arbroath was on his list of places to visit and they had arguably the best kippers in the world. He would eat the fishy delicacy there.

While he tucked into the sumptuous breakfast feast, he thought about what he needed to do next. The Joel Clement murder case was perplexing simply because there didn't appear to be a thread to pull at. Kate could not present an alibi and the evidence against her was convincing enough to secure a conviction: his fresh blood in the kitchen of their home, no sign of forced entry, no witnesses to anyone approaching Joel which might throw some doubt on her guilt. If there were some question about where Kate had been at the time of Joel's murder, or if there were a way to confirm she was home at the time of his disappearance, he might have a place to start. In theory, it might be possible to find someone who saw Joel after he left the pub, but to achieve that would either take a fat dollop of luck, or a massive number of manhours which he didn't have.

The police would have done that leg work if they were trying to find the killer. Officers would have been drafted in to support the local effort as they traced his last movements, but they hadn't done that. They'd gone straight to Kate.

Why?

Albert had to remind himself to continue chewing his breakfast because the question of what made the police go directly for Kate made him pause. It needed an answer, but he already suspected he knew what it was.

Rex popped up next to him, his tongue hanging over his bottom jaw as he panted with excitement. When Albert looked at him, the dog licked his lips and made solid eye contact.

'Give me the plate of eggs,' he commanded, doing his best to hypnotise his human. Much to his surprise, it worked, his human picking up the plate to place it on the floor in an absentminded way. The eggs didn't make it to the floor, Rex licked them off the plate in mid-air.

Satisfied that there was unlikely to be anything else until his human was finished with his breakfast, at which point Rex would highlight his extensive experience in cleaning plates, he laid back down to rest.

Albert powered through the rest of his meal, polishing off ninety-five percent of it even though, much like his clanger yesterday, there was truly more food than he required. His brain was sparking; messages flashing up to suggest one scenario or another. Something had sent the police sniffing

71

in Kate's direction, but in Albert's opinion, *something* was more likely to be someone and the pool of suspects was small.

Pushing his plate away, much to Rex's disgust, Albert stood up and patted his belly. Were his trousers tighter than they had been two weeks ago? He had to acknowledge that he was eating richer food than he might usually and drinking more alcohol. Well, it wasn't like he was going to live forever, and he had no aspirations to enter a swimsuit competition, so with another pat on his gut, he clicked his mouth at Rex and set out on his day.

His first stop was the pub's small reception area where he knew there to be a public phone, for those who didn't possess a mobile, he guessed, and an old-fashioned paper phone book which was what he wanted. How popular was the name Clement in this area? That was the first question to answer. Not very, it turned out, as there was only one entry. He couldn't tell if it was the right one, but he was prepared to give it a whirl. He didn't use the public phone in its cradle next to the phone book, nor his own mobile. He wanted to look into the person's eyes.

Albert wasn't sure what to expect, but the big, lavish house seemed to fit the bill. In front of the double garage, a nearly new Mercedes convertible sat waiting to be used. The detached family home had a wrought iron fence running from left and right to a pedestrian gate in the middle. The area between it and the house was solidly block paved, but there were large, ornate tubs with clipped trees along the front edge and at the leading edge of the house. Whoever spaced them, did so using a tape measure.

Going through the gate of Mrs Clement's property, Albert wondered how she had taken the news of her husband's death? He was here because someone had pointed the finger at Kate Harris. Eating his breakfast, his mind had flashed a case many years ago when, as a detective sergeant, he had wasted countless manhours pursuing a suspect and trying to make a conviction stick because of an anonymous tip off. They never did get to the bottom of who provided the tip, but it proved to be completely erroneous and he caught hell from the chief constable, a perfectionist who'd risen fast through the ranks and expected everyone to be able to match his record. Albert wracked his brain for a name, finally coming up with Quinn.

Albert nodded to himself as he gave the face in his memory a name: Harry Quinn, although Albert remembered most of the cops had a different name for the chief which they used when he was not around to hear it. Remembering him brought another memory to the surface, one where his son Randall had spoken about another fellow called Quinn. Apparently, Harry's grandson was making a name for himself in the Kent Police.

Approaching the door to what he believed was Mrs Clement's house, and planning to knock smartly on the door, Albert jumped when the door opened outwards. A trim, attractive woman in stretchy leggings and a figure-hugging top was equally startled to find a man on her doorstep.

They both recoiled, the woman almost slamming the door in fright and well might have had the person outside not be a kindly-looking old man with a dog.

'Mrs Clement?' Albert asked when his breath came back under control.

She raised one eyebrow. 'Not anymore. I recently remarried. What can I do for you?' Her instinct was to brush the man off; she was meeting friends at the gym and didn't want to be late. If he had an armful of leaflets, he'd have gotten a rude response and cold shoulder. Since he didn't, and didn't appear to be trying to sell anything, he got a few seconds of her time.

'My name is Albert Smith,' he introduced himself. 'And this is Rex.'

Rex sniffed the air, leaning forward to get a good noseful of the air coming from her house as the female human stood in the open doorway. He wasn't looking for anything in particular; truth was he didn't know where they were or who the female human was. There were no familiar smells he decided. The scent of the two men he wanted to find was not present so they had either never been here, or their visit was so long ago that their scent had long since faded.

'I'm investigating the circumstances of your husband, Joel's, death,' Albert explained.

'Ex-husband,' she reminded him. Albert chose to say husband on purpose, wondering how she might react. He was half expecting her to spit the words 'Ex-husband,' but she didn't. Her voice was calm and rational. 'You say investigating, yet, if you'll not think me rude, you look a little old to be a policeman.'

74

Albert chuckled. 'I am a little old, you are quite correct. I'm a little old to be most things, but I used to be a police officer. I apologise for dropping in unannounced like this, you see the police have Kate Harris in custody, I'm sure I don't need to tell you who that is.' He was prompting her to show her emotions. When he mentioned her ex-husband's death, she barely even blinked. Kate stole her man, wrecking the home and taking away the father to her children. She had moved on emotionally; time allows a person to do that, and she hadn't hung around in getting remarried. Surely though, the mention of Kate Harris would trigger a reaction.

The former Mrs Clement stared at him for a moment. 'Yes, I know who she is. I wasn't aware they had arrested her though. When did that happen?'

'Yesterday afternoon,' Albert supplied. 'If you'll pardon the observation, you appear very unmoved regarding your husband's murder, and even more so about the incarceration of the woman he left you for.'

Her eyes flared. 'You think he left me?' she faked a laugh. 'I kicked him out, the tubby, sweaty ball of lard. Honestly, I only married him because he got me pregnant at sixteen. I needed my head tested to have stayed with him as long as I did. All he ever did was eat.' She put her hands on her hips and pushed her shoulders back to accentuate her figure. 'Does it look like I eat too much?' Albert was struck dumb, unsure what answer he ought to give, but Mrs Clement wasn't finished. 'He never paid any attention to his own body but expected me to find him desirable. It was ridiculous.'

The revelation was a surprising slap to the face. He'd failed completely in his early assessment of the case, leaping to a conclusion that was entirely false. April accused Kate of being a homewrecker and he accepted it without question.

75

'I'm sorry,' he mumbled. 'I appear to have misjudged things. Someone pointed the finger at Kate Harris, I thought it might have been you.'

Mrs Clement laughed again, a high-pitched tinkling noise that sounded false. 'I have no quarrel with Kate Harris. I don't know the girl. I've seen her once or twice; she's rather plain looking, which makes her ideal for Joel. Or did, I should say. I can't imagine her killing him – he wasn't worth the effort.'

Albert nodded his head, giving Rex's lead a quick shake to make him get to his feet. 'I'll leave you to your day, Mrs ... um'

'Solomon,' she provided. She stepped out of her house, pulling the door shut behind her and making sure it was locked. 'I suppose I should wish you luck. I didn't love Joel. I don't think I ever did, but he didn't deserve to be murdered. If Kate didn't do it, then I hope you can clear her name.' It was the first heartfelt thing she had said in the five minutes he'd been on her doorstep.

By the time he made it back to the pavement beyond her property, her vehicle gate was sliding open and she pulled out and away without a glance in his direction. It felt like a wasted trip, but it wasn't. He'd been questioning his motivation for continuing given how many bad marks were stacking up against Kate. But now he had to view her in a different light. If she wasn't guilty of stealing a husband, what else wasn't she guilty of?

Accusation

The sky was darkening again, Albert's walk back through the town of Biggleswade one that was fraught with the danger of getting soaked to the bone if the heavens chose to open. He kept his pace as fast as he felt he could easily maintain and told his knees to stop creaking.

Rex was loving the outdoors, there were so many new smells to sample. This was so much more fun than sitting around in his human's house hoping for something interesting to happen. Before they came away, he would spend most of the day sleeping, and when he wasn't sleeping or hanging around the kitchen in the hope his human might drop something, he was patrolling the garden for the squirrel mafia, keeping his borders safe and his standards high. He wasn't going to be known as the dog in his village who couldn't keep the squirrels out. These things were okay to pass the time but not as interesting as the last few days had proven to be. He had been allowed to chase and bite people which was the best part, but in addition there had been things to eat, bowls of the tasty black stuff to drink that made his head go a bit swimmy, and they were out for walks all the time. It was great.

They were heading somewhere now, his human walking as if he had a purpose, but Rex couldn't work out if they were trying to solve a crime this time or not. He thought they were, but he hadn't smelled any blood, or … well anything his police handlers had taught him to alert for. He watched yesterday when a female human was taken away by the humans who wore uniforms and that was fine; he was used to that. It meant they'd found the person they were trying to find, the game was over, and he got to play with his ball. At least, that used to be what it meant. Of course, he hadn't been the one to find this particular human, so he hadn't earned the reward.

His human was up to something though; trying to uncover something but Rex didn't know what it was. He suspected the two men he'd smelled numerous times now were somehow involved in whatever it was; they were around and trying to stay out of sight. The concept made Rex chuckle; he loved that humans thought he couldn't find them if they went around a corner or hid under something. It demonstrated just how dumb humans were. They might be nothing to do with whatever his human was up to, but Rex found their behaviour suspicious and was keeping his nose alert for them.

Walking beside Rex, Albert was getting a niggling pain in his left hip. He rubbed at it with his hand but didn't let it slow him down. The draw of the unknown was pulling him onwards. That and the belief that he'd figured a part of this out now.

A church tower clock bonged to his right, a single clang of its giant bell. Albert was shocked that so much of the day had already slipped away. Visiting the police station, a late breakfast, and then walking everywhere had eaten through the morning. A quick check confirmed it was indeed one o'clock though either his watch was a little slow or the clock tower was a few minutes fast.

He was close enough to see the Clanger Café, the light coming through the front windows showing just how dim the sky was. Turning his collar up against a cool breeze which he felt certain was being pushed by a storm front, Albert made it to the café and into the beckoning warmth.

From under the door in the counter, Hans growled, 'You again?'

With his human making his way to the counter, Rex didn't rise to the bait. Instead he asked, 'Have the two humans been back in this morning? The ones we could smell following us.'

Hans had to think about his answer but confirmed he hadn't smelled them.

Above them, Albert was talking to a young lady behind the counter. 'Can I speak with Victor, please?' he asked.

The young woman, her age maybe eighteen or nineteen, Albert thought, showed surprise at the question. 'Um, he'll be in the kitchen,' she replied, looking over her shoulder and through the window into the back rooms.

A man in chef's whites came through the door at that point carrying a tray of clangers. 'More pork and cider,' he announced as another member of staff moved to unload the clangers to the glass display cabinet. He spoke more loudly than was necessary and his reason for it was obvious: there was a heated discussion raging in the backrooms and the raised voices carried through the door with him.

A dozen customers' heads lifted to see where the argument came from, and the man with the tray of clangers pulled an embarrassed face. 'It's about to go nuclear in there,' he muttered to the two members of staff within earshot. Albert was close enough to hear what he said, and close enough to recognise that the argument was between Victor and April.

'I'm here to see Victor,' Albert announced. 'It's about his sister and I think he needs to hear what I have to say right now.'

Albert thought the staff were going to argue for a moment, but the man sagged with relief. His tray empty, he placed it on a rack behind him and moved to the counter's swing door. 'Please,' he beckoned Albert to come through. 'Anything to shut those two up. They've been at it for an hour. Well, ever since April …' the man waved his arm, searching for the right words, but gave up and said, 'I'll let you see for yourself.'

Led through to the back office where Albert checked over the books yesterday evening, he could have found them just by following the noise. It was mostly Victor doing the shouting, April's responses were, for the most part, delivered in a calm manner. Pausing just outside the door, Albert whispered his thanks to the chef and chose to listen rather than interrupt the fight going on inside. However, a quick glance around the doorframe to see the two persons inside, instantly revealed what had Victor so hot under the collar.

April was wearing a suit. It was a skirt suit and looked brand new as if she had purposefully got it this morning or perhaps last night. They discovered Joel Clement had been killed three days ago, so however she came by it, she leapt on the opportunity before his body was even cold. The suit was a clear indication that she saw herself in the management role, but to chase away any ambiguity, on her left lapel she wore a badge which read April Saunders, Manager.

'You have no position of authority!' ranted Victor. Albert suspected he might have made that point several times already. 'You cannot just declare yourself king and steal the throne. We work as a team here. Kate is the owner now, she will decide who runs the café, and I expect it will be her.'

'Kate is on her way to jail,' smirked April, making a joke out of Victor's claims. 'She's no more owner than her stupid little dog. That's another thing I will be changing. No dogs in the café.'

'He never goes in the kitchen,' Victor protested, failing to see that acknowledging her argument gave her more power.

'He'll not be coming onto the premises from today. I want him gone within the hour,' snapped April.

'You are not in charge!' Victor shouted. 'You have no position to demand or dictate anything!'

April's voice was at normal conversation volume when she delivered her next line. 'You're a good baker, Victor, but that doesn't mean you are irreplaceable. You will need to watch your attitude if you hope to keep your position here.'

Victor screamed his frustration to the sky. 'You can't hire and fire either, you daft cow!'

'That's it!' she growled. 'I won't take that kind of behaviour from my staff. You're fired.'

Albert heard a sound, a fast shuffling of feet, and worried it might be Victor moving to throttle the older woman, he stepped into the room. His sudden appearance in the room surprised both occupants, but Victor wasn't moving to attack April, he was thumping his head against the wall.

'Who allowed you to come back here?' snarled April, her stern expression well at home on her face. 'I'll have their job too. Look at that dog! It's unhygienic, that's what it is. Victor, see him out.'

'Really, April. I thought I was fired,' Victor pointed out. He turned toward Albert, but reversed direction to deliver a parting message to the crazy woman in her power suit. 'I'm going back to work. I don't care what you do, but any orders you attempt to give will be countered by my own. The staff won't fall into line behind you. You might not have noticed, April, but they don't like you. Nobody likes you. You are a malodorous old bag.'

'Popularity is not a requirement of leadership, Victor. If you were management material, you would know that,' she countered with a smile, his insults failing to even register.

He'd been trying to end the argument, but it was back in full swing again. 'Popularity might not be required, but respect is!' he shouted, anger making him raise his voice. 'You have neither. Which when we add it to the FACT,' he hit the word hard, 'that you have no authority, makes you the one most likely to be leaving the business.'

'Kate isn't coming back, Victor,' April stated confidently. 'The courts will nullify her ownership because she lured Joel into making her a partner. That will leave the business adrift.'

Albert watched the interplay, listening to April's words with interest to see if she would give anything away, but he'd heard enough and was ready to interrupt now.

'Actually, that's not how it will work at all,' said Albert loudly enough to get April's attention. A shuffling noise made him glance to his right where he spotted members of staff listening in from around the corner. 'If Kate Harris is convicted, it will be in a criminal court. Criminal courts are not interested in property or business ownership. A civil case would have to be raised to prove Kate obtained ownership of this café by unfair means. That is a lengthy and longwinded process and then who would the ownership pass to?'

April rolled her eyes. 'The manager of the business. Isn't it obvious?'

Victor's jaw fell open. 'So that's it! You don't just want to run this place. You think you can steal it out from under everyone!'

Albert delivered the line he'd been holding in reserve. It was a bomb, and now felt like the moment to drop it. 'Is that why you made an anonymous call to the police, April? It was you who told them Kate Harris killed Joel Clement.'

The room – the whole café – fell silent.

Albert let the dust from his accusation settle for a few seconds, waiting for April to draw a breath as she readied her response. He expected a denial, but he didn't give her the chance. The moment she looked like she might speak, he rolled right over the top of her. 'I checked,' he lied. 'The call didn't come with a name, but the dispatcher logged it and described the person's voice. Did you know that when you make a 999 call, they are recorded?' he took out his phone. 'Would you like to hear the call you made?'

April's face was like thunder. It was a dangerous game to play, but he'd been confident that the police must have gone after Kate when someone told them to. Randall had confirmed that, but Albert didn't have a description of the voice and certainly didn't have a recording of the call on his phone. He'd bluffed her, but he did so because her eyes betrayed her fear when he levelled the accusation at her.

Snatching up her handbag, April threw some items into it. 'You shall be hearing from my lawyer!' Albert didn't give her threat much credence. 'Kate Harris is guilty of murder and she is guilty of stealing from this business.' April had looked like she was about to storm from the room, but Albert's accusation had drawn the staff around the corner to come to the office door. With an audience, April chose to reveal what she knew. 'Here!' she railed. 'Look at the accounts! Your beloved Kate has been pilfering from the till for months and doing her best to cover it up. Once a criminal, always a criminal.' She stepped away from the screen, hooking her left arm through the loops of her handbag as she stormed for the office door. 'This place will fall apart without me to run it. Let's see how long you can manage without me! You'll be begging me to come back!' her voice echoed through the building. 'Begging!' her final shout was followed by the sound of a door slamming and the café was quiet again.

No one said anything for a few seconds.

Rex had been listening to the humans shouting at each other but hadn't found it interesting. He couldn't keep up with what was being said and they hadn't mentioned food, walkies, or ball at any point, so he'd stopped bothering to listen. There was a rubbish bin in the corner behind the desk that had an apple core in it and a wrapper from a packet of chocolate digestives. There was some chocolate still inside the wrapper unless his nose was wrong – which it never was. However, he doubted it was worth the effort to retrieve.

Hans wandered through to find where all the humans had got to. 'What's going on?' he asked Rex, foregoing his obligatory need to lead with an insult.

Rex sniffed the air. 'Nothing interesting. Something is burning though.' From a sitting position he jumped to his feet and barked. The sudden noise made everyone jump but before anyone had a chance to ask why the dog was barking, the smoke alarm burst into life.

Victor swore and he wasn't the only one. April and the dodgy accounting were swiftly forgotten as the staff ran back to the kitchen which, by the time Albert got there, was filling with smoke. No one needed to take charge, not right away at least, the fire alarm and all the shouting before it had scared away all the customers. Anyone coming through the café front door now would swiftly turn around.

Albert coughed as acrid smoke caught in his throat and that was enough to convince him it was time to leave. A tray of clangers had been left to burn, that was the source of the smoke, the cause nothing more than curiosity as whoever should have been tending to them, drifted away to listen to April and Victor. It would be easily dealt with, but the café would be shut for the rest of the day, Albert felt certain of that.

Holding his breath until he got to the door, Albert's pulse was beginning to hammer when he sucked in a lungful of cool, moist air. He was jostled in the doorway and hadn't thought anyone was following him. Trying to get out of the way, he heard Victor's voice and turned toward it, getting rewarded with a lump pressed into his arms.

'Can you look after Hans while I deal with this?' The lump in his arms was the dachshund, who looked bewildered and was coughing. Victor shouted, 'Thanks,' as he ran back through the café to the kitchen. He hadn't waited for an answer.

Albert looked down at his new charge. 'Hello, Hans.'

Hans looked up, letting his tongue loll out as he greeted the old man. 'I'm way better than a German Shepherd. You'll soon be phoning the pound to drop off the stupid brute you've got so you can get a cool dog like me instead.'

Rex growled a warning.

'Don't go getting jealous now, Rex,' Albert chided his dog. 'I'm just holding him because we don't have his lead with us.'

'Yeah, that and because I'm adorable,' cheered Hans, wriggling around until he was lying on his back and being cradled like a baby.

Rex growled again.

Albert had to wait ten minutes before Victor returned. Someone had come out to prop the front door open, using a chair which Albert then helpfully sat on to keep it in place. The doors and windows at the back were also open, the passage of air driving the smoke from the café as the staff cleaned up the mess.

'What a mess,' muttered Victor, sagging against the doorframe. 'Would you like a free clanger? It may or may not be flavoured by the smoke.' Victor pointed to the glass cabinet set into the counter which was mostly full of clangers waiting to be sold. 'I've got about a day's worth of product going to waste now. I can't sell it, and we'll have to air the café out for the rest of the day to make sure it doesn't smell when we open tomorrow morning. It's just one thing after another at the moment.' He sighed, a weary, mournful noise that captured how he felt without the need for words. 'I wonder if the café can survive this.'

He didn't expect a response to his statement and Albert didn't offer one. He was thinking about what he did want to eat as a smoke flavoured clanger did not appeal. He was also pondering what he could or should do next. Having established that the police focussed their attention on Kate because April fingered her for the crime, he understood how the current situation came about. However, he hadn't gained any useful knowledge. Kate still had no alibi and all the motive. No one else had presented themselves as a viable suspect to investigate – he didn't for one moment think April was guilty – so what was his next move? It already felt like he was clutching at straws.

Sucking on his lips in thought, he decided that if all he had to clutch at were straws, he might as well accept it and see what fruit they might bear. 'Do you, by any chance, have a key to your sister's house?'

Victor didn't have a key, but he knew where Kate kept her spare. Returning from a quick trip to the accountancy office in the back of the building, he also had Hans's lead in his hand when he got back.

'Can you keep Hans with you for a little while, please?' he begged.

Rex couldn't believe his ears. Nor his eyes, when they set off together, Hans straining his lead to be the dog in front even though he was one quarter Rex's length.

Victor needed to keep the café doors open and didn't want to lock Hans in one of the backrooms where he might start chewing things. Albert didn't think Hans would do that, chewing destructively is something dogs grow out of when they are still puppies, but he thought it might do Rex good to have a doggy friend around for a while.

'I can't believe you are coming with us,' muttered Rex.

Hans sniggered. 'Worried you might get replaced?'

'By you? Be serious. My human likes to have a dog by his side, not a handbag accessory,'

'Hey!' yelled Albert as the dachshund threw his snapping teeth at Rex's front paws. After that, he kept them both on short leads and to either side of him, positioning himself in the middle. 'I don't care which one of you started it.' he chastised them both equally. 'I'll be the one who finishes it.'

When he came across a public house, Albert didn't think twice about going inside. It was one he had passed on his way into the town the day he arrived, and it boasted Bedfordshire's finest selection of craft ciders. Albert usually drank stout if he were to have a longer drink, or sometimes a lager if he wanted to drink it quickly. Today, a cider sounded tempting, but more than anything, he needed a rest.

Failing to observe the dull aches creeping into his legs, hips, and back would only result in feeling too sore to do anything tomorrow. He was keen to get to Kate's but would be good to no one if he wore himself out.

In the pub, he ended up with Hans on his lap. This was partly to keep the two dogs apart because they wouldn't stop growling at each other, and partly because the dog was jumping up and wagging his tail to be picked up.

'See,' Hans goaded Rex, 'You're already second fiddle, wolf.'

Rex narrowed his eyes and curled back his top lip. He was going to get even with the dachshund soon enough. Until then, he laid himself on the wooden floor and closed his eyes to consider his possible methods of revenge.

After sampling his pint of cold, crisp, apple cider, Albert busied himself with a call to his eldest son, Gary.

'Dad,' said Gary when he answered the phone.

With the immediate impression that his son was too busy to talk, Albert said, 'I'm just checking in, son. If you are busy at work, you can call me back when it's more convenient to you.'

'No, now is as good of a time as any. Are you still expecting to arrive in York on time?'

Albert was supposed to be leaving Biggleswade today and was yet to speak with the pub landlord about staying on an extra night. However, given the time, he had to accept it was already impractical to travel to York today.

'I think I will stay another night here, actually. It's rather nice,' he said, opting to give an answer that was wholly true while also avoiding the truth.

There was silence at the other end for a beat until Gary said, 'You've got a case to investigate, haven't you? Has that brother of mine been helping you again? Selina has been off with sick kids and you haven't asked me for anything, unless that's what this call is for.'

'Not at all, son,' Albert protested.

'Then it's Randall,' concluded Gary, passing sentence on his younger brother. 'What bother are you getting into this time, Dad?'

Albert blew out a frustrated breath. 'No bother, Gary. There's just a wrongfully accused woman and I am looking to see if I can find the real killer.'

'Killer!' blurted his eldest son. 'Oh, my God, Dad. You're interfering with a murder investigation!'

Getting grumpy, and wishing he hadn't made the call, Albert defended himself. 'I'm not interfering. I'm just looking around a bit. You did read about the thing in Stilton, right?' Albert felt his children were too harsh with him. To his mind, he'd been rather successful of late.

However, Gary saw a chance to hammer home his point. 'If you mean, did I read about your dog wrecking the cheese rolling race, then yes, I did. And I saw it on television. And I found an A3 poster of you chasing Rex as he ran off with a whole Stilton in his mouth. It was stuck to my desk when I came to work two days ago, and I haven't found the culprit yet.'

Albert couldn't stop himself from sniggering. It hadn't been funny at the time, but when he watched the footage on the news that night – it made the national ten o'clock BBC broadcast as a human interest snippet - he'd been unable to stop himself from laughing.

Gary was about to get upset, so Albert quashed his mirth, saying, 'I just called to check in, Gary. I'll see you in York in two days.'

Albert got another sigh in response. 'Yes, Dad. Two days. I'm coming in on the midday rocket from London; a two-hour straight shot from Kings Cross to York.'

'I'll meet you at the station,' Albert volunteered. 'I expect there will be a bar or a coffee shop nearby where I can wait with Rex.'

The phone call ended, and Albert finished his tall glass of cider. In retrospect he probably should have opted for tea or coffee or maybe even a hot chocolate. The temperature was dipping outside; it was a cold autumn day with a stiff breeze kicking the leaves along the street and forming eddies at the edge of buildings where they would dance as if engaging in a game.

Kate's house was right across town, the directions Victor gave easy enough to follow so he walked right to it without needing to back track. In his long police career, Albert had only needed to force entry to a property on three occasions. Doing so in an urban environment always attracted the attention of neighbours who would call the police as an immediate response. Without a key, he wouldn't have dreamed of trying to get into Kate's property. He'd thought about having a look around it many hours ago; it was an obvious place to explore since Joel had possibly been taken from here and Kate was accused of not being here when she claimed to be. Albert's expectation was that he would come later with Victor, but this worked too.

Using the key, he let himself in, strolling up the path as if he belonged there. If a neighbour saw him, he didn't think they would call the police, but if they did, he had a key and permission to be inside the premises.

Albert had to nudge Rex to get him inside because he's stopped halfway across the threshold. Then he left the dogs, unclipping each from their leads so they could explore while he methodically inspected the house for clues.

Rex froze the moment the door opened. The humans had been here, the ones who were in the café yesterday and following them this morning. He sucked in a big sample of air, holding it as he broke the scents down and filed them away. There was no mistaking it, no question in his mind. As he understood it, a human had been killed and Han's human, the female one, was taken away by the police for doing it. He'd never been able to bend his head around humans' need to kill each other. Kill for food, yes. Protect your territory, yes, and he accepted that in the course of protecting one's territory, it might be necessary to kill. However, humans would just bump each other off for no good reason at all. A lot of it seemed to revolve around mating and that was just bonkers.

Rex understood the desire to mate; it was hardwired into him much the same as every other living thing on the planet. Humans made it unnecessarily complicated. Smell available female, go to available female, if female is with another dog, either wait turn or fight dog. Then, get the job done, move on, and forget what the female even smelled like because you can already smell another available female. What was so hard about that?

Pushing his thoughts on the obscurity of human behaviour to one side, he needed to tell his human about the two humans who had been here.

Albert had wandered to the kitchen at the back of the house. From memory, the detective claimed there was blood found there – another mark against Kate. He couldn't see it, but Kate would have cleaned it up whether guilty or not. Cleaning it wouldn't prevent the crime scene chaps from finding it; they did such things with clever scopes these days. He was about to start opening drawers when Rex found him.

'What is it, Rex?' His dog was making bark/whine noises at him in an excited way again. It was clear the dog wanted to impart a message, but Albert could not decipher what the sounds Rex made were supposed to mean. He tried to guess, 'You can smell gravy bones and think you are overdue a treat?'

'Did someone say gravy bones?' asked Hans, skidding to a stop, and barking gleefully. 'They are in that cupboard there.'

Rex licked his lips and tried again. 'There were two bad men here. They were in the café yesterday and outside it again last night. Plus, they were following us, or maybe Hans and the other human he was with this morning.'

'Gravy bone, yes?' said Albert, his voice taking on an excited edge to see if Rex would react and let him know he was on the right track.

'That cupboard there!' squealed Hans. 'Right there!'

Albert started opening cupboards, certain Kate wouldn't mind that he'd fed her dog a biscuit.

'No, right there,' barked Hans, pointing his head and eyes at the right door and wondering why the human was looking everywhere else.

'Ah, here we are.' Albert found a box of dog biscuits and doled out one each.

Rex was miffed that he couldn't get his human to listen to his clear and simple message and knew that if he took the gravy bone, which he dearly wanted, the old man would assume he'd got it right and that would be that. He turned his nose up at the treat and focussed his gaze on his human's eyes.

Hans, having scoffed his biscuit in under a second, snatched the other one the man still held in his hand and started crunching that too.

'Hey!' snarled Rex, swearing under his breath. The dachshund was licking up crumbs when Rex moved his front right paw and accidentally trod on the smaller dog's left ear. Pinning his head in place, Rex then leaned his weight that way to ensure the dog couldn't move and the old man couldn't see him. 'Now, where was I? Oh yes, I remember. OPEN YOUR NOSE!' he barked loud enough to make his human jump. 'You've got two humans following us around and a human who was murdered. They were all in this house together!'

'What's got into you, Rex?'

Han's couldn't get his ear out from under Rex's paw and couldn't turn his head to bite him either. His only option was to let out a soulful whine, the type a human couldn't hope to resist.

'You're standing on Hans.' Albert had to get hold of Rex's shoulder and shove him backwards. Even then, Rex tried to keep his paw in place on top of the dachshund's ear.

'Keep pushing your luck, sausage,' he growled, watching Hans play the part of the wounded dog. Hans was clinging to Rex's human as the old man lifted the smaller dog into the air for a cuddle.

'Am I going to have to shut you in the garden?' Albert asked, looking down at Rex with an accusing stare.

'Me?' Rex couldn't believe his ears. 'You think I'm the one to blame. Well, that's just perfect. I hope the two of you will be very happy together.' Angry that the dachshund was winning, Rex took himself out of the kitchen to wait by the front door. He didn't want to have to look at his human giving the annoying sausage dog the affection which Rex felt was rightfully his.

'Did the nasty big dog hurt you?' Albert asked Hans, getting a lick on his chin in reply. 'Yes, I bet he did. What a brute he is.'

Albert's baby talk as he petted Hans reached Rex's ears as he sat facing the inside of the front door. If they were at home, or even back in their room at the pub, it would be one of those occasions where he accidentally widdled in a certain someone's shoes.

Albert put Hans down to continue his search. There had to be something here that would exonerate Kate. If she had been here alone all evening waiting for Joel to get home, then surely there would be some evidence to prove she hadn't driven her lover's body to Wales.

He found a tower computer. Unable to tell if it was hers or Joel's, it didn't really matter because he doubted he would be able to access it. However, he had to wonder if Kate had maybe used it on the evening in question. Would a computer forensic scientist be able to prove that it was Kate using the machine?

To get an answer, he called Randall.

'Hey, Randall,' he jumped in as soon as he heard his son's voice. 'If a person were using their computer, doing social media whatnot and the like, could one of the forensics guys tell who was using it just from the profile being accessed?' Albert wasn't certain he had the terminology right. He didn't do social media; to him it was all a bit odd to be sharing everything with everyone, but he expected Randall would understand what he meant.

'You mean look at entry of passwords and the keystroke record to determine that the messages on a person's social profile were sent from a particular computer? Yeah, sure. No one under the age of fifty uses a computer to do that though, Dad. Everyone uses their phone. Plus, if I understand your question, you want to prove a person was in a certain place when the messages were sent but that won't work.'

Grimacing because his ray of hope had proved so fleeting, Albert asked, 'Why not?'

'Because it would only show that the computer was the one used. It wouldn't prove who used it. Passwords can be obtained, or even shared willingly. It would never stand up in court.'

Disappointed, Albert thanked Randall for taking the call and disconnected. He moved on, poking in the waste bin, then lifting the lid to get a better look. He found takeaway cartons amid the torn-up envelopes, apples cores, and teabags. Going through bins could yield results but he wasn't of a mood to try that now. He opened drawers and poked in cupboards, scratched his head, and tried to think of things that would show she was here and not somewhere else murdering Joel Clement.

He finished his tour of the house in the master bedroom. Feeling like a peeping tom as he went through her underwear drawer, he was now sitting on the foot of the bed and wondering what to do. After an hour of searching, he'd accepted defeat: it was time to try something else.

The only problem with that approach was that he couldn't come up with anything else to try. Trudging back down the stairs, he found Rex still facing the front door though the dog had laid down at some point and was asleep. Hans was on the couch, most likely in his usual spot, and fast asleep also.

'Come along, dogs. I think it's time we checked on the café and Victor. Maybe he is nearly finished.' Hans opened an eye but didn't move. Further encouragement by Albert only succeeded in getting the dachshund to open his other eye. He was comfortable and saw no reason to go outside. It was getting dark and it smelled like the rain was back.

Unable to get the sausage dog to move, Albert went to him, clipping the lead to his collar and then lifting him from the couch to the floor where the dog finally gave in and started using his paws. Rex was on his feet, keen to leave having had enough of being ignored by his human. There would be a reckoning later, or there would be an edible treat of sufficient value for his human to earn forgiveness. Rex wasn't sure which he hoped for most.

Albert paused in the doorway, making sure he had all the things he came in with, especially the spare key to Kate's house which he had to search for. It was in his right front trouser pocket, buried beneath a folded handkerchief.

With a dog lead in each hand, he set off back to the centre of town. The rain was back, but it was fine misty droplets. Enough to dampen his clothing and leave a sheen on the dogs' coats. But not enough to make him hurry.

More than a mile ahead of him, Victor was getting ready to lock up. He and the rest of his colleagues at the café had done the best they could. It had been a testing week with one thing and another, a fire in the bakery was really just the cherry on top of what had been a run of terrible events they all wanted to forget.

Someone joked that if bad luck ran in threes, they were already onto number four or five depending on how one chose to count. Someone else commented that April storming out was a good luck omen not bad. With a vote to go to the pub as they were forced to close the café early and they felt it was needed, the crowd of café staff trudged away through the rain which was beginning to pick up its pace.

Victor stayed behind to lock up, promising to meet them there in a few minutes and placing his beverage request. Across the courtyard behind the café, once the staff had rounded the corner, a muscular shadow in combat fatigues detached from the wall and held a weapon aloft.

The rain was beginning to come in sideways by the time Albert made it back to the B road that ran through the centre of town. It was late afternoon and the sun had all but set, making the temperature drop yet further. At the edge of the road, he had to wait for a gap in the traffic before he could cross and got even wetter from the rain being splashed up by the passing cars. Heavy trucks and vans were among the cars going past, reminding Albert of back home before they built the Kings Hill bypass. This town clearly needed a ring road too.

Both dogs had their heads down, hiding their faces from the rain and powering on to wherever they were going while hoping it would be somewhere dry. Periodically, one of the dogs would pause a step to shake their coat, ejecting a shower of water onto the pavement all around them but also onto Albert's legs so he now had one very wet left ankle from Hans and one very wet right outer thigh and calf where Rex's superior height and coat length had ejected water that hit everything on the side up to and including his eyebrows. Discouraging Rex from shaking himself seemed to just make the dog do it more as if he were purposefully lining himself up to get Albert wet.

Rex was muttering under his breath. It was the second day in a row he'd been taken for a walk in driving rain. Once was bad enough; the second time was just an insult and it came on top of a bevy of insults already delivered. At least the rain was getting the dachshund too who was having a devil of a time trying to avoid the puddles which were over the top of his paws in places.

Wishing he had timed things a little better, Albert pressed on. The option to seek refuge in a public house until the rain passed or eased was no longer viable – he was just too wet. He would have to drop Hans back with Victor and carry on to his room in the Leather Bottle. There he could get dry and find a change of clothes. The investigation was supposed to be a welcome distraction, not a chore, and that was how it was beginning to feel. Rex was soaked he could see and that meant he would have to beg the landlord for some old towels once they got inside. He dared not take the shaggy-coated dog up to his room until he was dry; the mess Rex made in the café yesterday stood a stark warning.

The light in the café was off when they turned the final corner and could see its frontage. In fact, there was no sign of life at all. Albert skewed his lips to one side in thought; he might have to call Victor. Had the man gone home after his day too tired to remember Hans?

At the entry door, both dogs waited for Albert to push it open, Rex twisting his head around to glance up when they remained outside.

Albert gave the door an experimental push but, as expected, it was locked, the closed sign not there just to tease him. 'I think we'll have to go around the back and try there, chaps,' he said aloud as rain continued to drip from his head down past his collar. The top of his shirt and sweater were already soaked.

He didn't know how to get around to the back, and when a glance to his left and right revealed no clues, he guessed. Thanking the Lord that he got it right first time, he found a narrow passage that led around to the rear of the parade of shops. It passed between two premises to reach a courtyard behind. Albert hoped to find a sign of life in the back offices, but as he entered the small loading and car park area, his eyes were drawn to the two men putting Victor through the side door of their van.

A pregnant pause ensued where the two men, one holding Victor's arms, the other his legs, looked at Albert and Albert looked at them. Victor was completely limp and therefore unconscious or possibly dead.

Albert hoped for the former over the latter but had no way of knowing which it might be.

The men were dressed very differently to each other. One wore dark combat fatigues but even in the dim light behind the shops where there were no streetlights, Albert could see the other man had on a jacket, shirt, and tie. It was the well-dressed man who spoke first, yelling, 'Get him!' as he flung Victor's limp body into the van. The other man wasn't as fast to react, failing to throw Victor's feet so their victim flopped half in and half out of the van and then fell out onto the wet ground as gravity took over.

Rex's ears were up the moment they came around the corner and he could smell the two humans. 'It's them,' he murmured to himself, sniffing the air and looking with his eyes as he tried to pinpoint their location. The rain was playing havoc with his olfactory system; sniffing deeply meant getting a load of water up his nose which then made him sneeze. He hadn't been paying attention either; too grumpy to bother until the familiar scent smacked him in the nose.

A car blocked his view, but when Hans started barking and snapping, and Rex's human shouted, 'Rex go!' he didn't need to know where they were to know that it was time to attack. They had to be ahead of him somewhere, so the moment the tension in his lead came free, he leapt onto the bonnet of the car that blocked his view, and there they were; two humans, with a third human he knew lying on the ground between their feet.

Oh, yeah! It was chase and bite time.

Eugene had just started forward, breaking into a sprint to get the old man because he couldn't see the dog. He got two paces before the dog jumped onto the front of a BMW and was very suddenly staring right at his face. Eugene swore loudly and reversed direction, his feet slipping on the tarmac as he tried to fight his inertia.

He went down to the ground, landing painfully, but he saw the dog leap and had no time to question if he was hurt. He needed to get into the van right now. He had a knife there, tucked into the cubby hole under the dash. He knew he ought to keep it on his person, but it spoiled the line of his jacket.

'I've got this one, wolf!' yelled Hans, whipping around the side of the car to find Eugene on the ground. He could see Victor – a human he knew well – lying on the wet ground and he could smell his familiar scent. He didn't understand what was happening, but a primal instinct told him he needed to attack now.

Francis was getting away. He was still dropping Victor's feet when the giant dog appeared and got to see Eugene fall. It was clear his colleague wouldn't be able to get away before the dog got to him, so he used that to his advantage, sacrificed Eugene willingly, and ran. All he had to do was get around the other side of the van and into the driver's seat. He would drive away, escape the town, and ditch the van in a multi-story carpark somewhere. Eugene would get caught by the police, but he wouldn't talk.

Rex jumped down to the ground. The human on the ground was helpless now. He could bite and tear but the shout from Hans changed his mind. The tiny dog might be a handbag accessory, but he was still a dog with two rows of teeth and therefore better than any human. He leapt over the stricken Eugene to pursue the other human who had just vanished around the back of the van.

Hans had never bitten a human before. It was a concept disciplined out of him when he was very young. So young, in fact, that he didn't remember it, only that it was a terrible thing for a dog to do. Now was the right time to overrule that instruction which he did by sinking his teeth into the human's ankle as he tried to get up.

Eugene cried out in pain. He saw the German Shepherd coming and shut off every other thought other than escape. He had to get to the van! When the bite came, he'd been telling himself to expect it and to fight to get free. He could be stitched up later, but there was something wrong with the bite he felt and when he swung his free leg around to kick the large dog away, it connected with thin air.

Hans ripped his head from side to side, yanking at the human's flesh and growling for all he was worth. He would show the wolf just what a smaller dog was capable of.

On the other side of the van, Francis grabbed the driver's door handle, yanked it open and dove inside. He tugged the door closed and whipped his feet out of the way so it would slam shut. Half a heartbeat later, something heavy smashed into the other side of the door.

He'd made it! Now he could get out of here, running the old man and the dog over if he got a chance. Francis had no idea where Eugene had gone. Since the dog was chasing him, it clearly hadn't gone after Eugene, so why wasn't his partner in the van?

When the dog's head appeared at the driver's side window, barking insanely and suggesting that he might bite through the glass or just rip the door open with its teeth if he hung around, Francis gave up on Eugene and grabbed for the ignition key.

It wasn't there!

Outside on the wet ground, Eugene rolled around so he could look down the length of his body. It wasn't the great brute of a German

Shepherd at all. He was being mauled by a sausage dog! It hurt like the blazes, but if Francis saw him, he'd never live it down.

Hans threw his body from side to side again, but so focussed in his efforts was he, that he failed to see the human lining up to kick him. The boot caught his right shoulder, shooting him across the carpark and into a barrel roll as he lost control and chose to go with it. He landed right way up, and though he felt dizzy and disorientated, he flipped back onto his feet and ran back into the fight.

Eugene was moving the moment the dog's teeth left his flesh. Driving up from the ground like a sprinter coming out of their blocks, he had only a scant handful of yards to cover to get to the van and safety. Stuff the earl's instructions to bring Victor Harris back. He could send someone else. This mission was a bust already.

In the van, Francis looked around hopelessly. He needed the key and his stupid partner, Eugene, probably had them in the pocket of his trousers. What on Earth was his next move? The dog was still barking like crazy and the old man was on his phone; Francis could see it illuminating the old man's face at the edge of the courtyard. It didn't take a genius to work out that the police would be here soon. Where on Earth was Eugene with the keys?

Rex had hurt his face when he slammed into the van's closing door, but the taste of blood in his mouth was just fuelling his desire to bite someone. He barked threats and promises at the human just inches away on the other side of the glass, but he couldn't get to him. Or so the human clearly thought, but when Rex spied an opportunity, he stopped barking and started running again.

Eugene slammed into the passenger's side of the van, fumbling for the door handle now slippery with rain and the mud and crud on his fingers.

He'd given the little dachshund a mighty kick to its head, sending it five yards across the carpark. His intention had been to kill it with one blow, but the tough little blighter was already coming back for seconds; barking and growling his evil intentions. Eugene figured he had about a second and a half before the dog was on his ankle again and it was already sticky with blood from the last attack. Maybe if Francis hadn't seen it, he could say it was a bulldog; those are low to the ground too, but a mite tougher sounding than a sausage dog.

He ripped the door open, landing inside in the dry, safe interior. He was out of breath and shaking from the adrenalin surging through his body, but he hadn't expected Francis to grab his lapels before his backside had even come to rest on the seat.

'Where are the keys?' screamed Francis, getting into Eugene's face. He wanted to know where his fool partner had been but there was no time for a Q and A session. They needed to leave now!

Sensing the urgency Francis felt, Eugene squirmed around to get his hand into his trouser pocket but came up empty. This started a frantic patting session as he explored all the possible places the keys might be, certain in his head that he'd put the keys in his front right trouser pocket where he always kept them.

'Come on!' yelled Francis, but a worried glance showed them both where the keys were: they were outside on the ground in the rain.

'They must have fallen out when the dog got me!' Eugene wailed in despair.

Francis couldn't believe his idiot colleague had the nerve to make up excuses. 'The dog was chasing me, not you! What were you doing?'

Eugene growled, 'There're two dogs!' But just as he said that, Hans whipped through a pool of light on his way to the van and Francis coughed out a laugh.

'That thing? That's what got you? Good thing it wasn't a gerbil, it might have had your leg off!' despite their situation, he found the sausage dog attack truly funny. That was until they both felt the van's suspension dip and all thoughts of mirth and counterargument evaporated when they turned to see Rex behind them.

They'd left the side door open!

With a scream, both men went out their respective doors so fast it defied the laws of physics. Rex's teeth closed with a snap in the space Francis's neck had occupied mere moments before, and the door slammed in his face when he tried to follow.

Eugene and Francis found themselves back in the carpark. The van's keys were tantalisingly close, but they stood no chance of getting to them before both dogs were upon them. The surprisingly loud dachshund was coming up fast and the big dog would be out of the van in seconds. There was nothing for it: they were going to have to go on foot.

The vehicle exit from the courtyard was to their left, directly opposite where the old man stood. Francis took off running, yelling for Eugene to follow. If they could get to the road, maybe they could stop someone and steal their car. Maybe they could find a wall to climb and escape that way. All he knew was that he needed to go right now.

Seeing Francis sprint for the way out and the road beyond, Eugene followed him, but his right ankle was sore enough that it stopped him running flat out as Francis was.

Rex came out of the van with his body already changing direction in mid-air. His front paws met the tarmac and drove off as he leaned into the bend and got himself around the front of the van. Hans was already running at full speed, whipping by Rex as he too pursued the two men.

His human was shouting something; Rex could hear his name being called but he only needed a few seconds to bring his quarry down now. They were in the open and on foot. There was nowhere for them to go and no hope of escape now. This was the best part, so far as Rex was concerned. Afterwards, the humans could work out who had done what and why. All he needed to know was that the humans he was chasing had done something wrong and he got to be the one to stop them.

His longer stride meant he would catch up to and overtake Hans in a few paces. He was coming up to full speed, just a few more bounds and he would be able to leap. The nearest human was hobbling a little. Rex planned to bring him down and then go after the other one. But with a gut-wrenching twist, he saw the danger and altered his plan.

Francis was running flat out, his arms and legs pumping as he hit the pavement. He was on the B road that ran through the town and Eugene was hot on his heels. The dogs were too close for him to hope to jack a car, but the moving traffic presented a different opportunity. There was no hope of timing it, he just had to go and hope for the best. Francis reached the edge of the pavement and kept going, zipping out in front of a truck laden with asphalt for the new ring-road being built around the town.

The driver swore and slammed on his brakes.

Rex caught up to Hans, sideswiping the smaller dog with a paw to alter his trajectory and send him crashing to the ground.

Francis ripped through the gap, narrowly missing the truck's front bumper just as he intended. Anything following too closely behind didn't stand a chance. Unfortunately for Eugene, that meant him.

Just as Hans skittered across the pavement and Rex did everything he could to stop himself, the man they were chasing was hit by the truck. Rex had seen it from the corner of his eye and knew the chase was doomed. He couldn't get to the men, but he could save the dachshund from certain death.

Eugene landed more than ten yards down the road, hitting a lamppost with a sickening crunch that left a dent in the galvanised steel. His body spun through a horizontal plane and landed face down in the gutter. He didn't move.

When the men ran from the dark courtyard with the dogs tearing after them, Albert had screamed for them to stop. He could see the men were heading toward the busy main road and fear gripped him for what might happen if the dogs tried to follow them across it. Neither dog showed any sign of even hearing him and he could do nothing but watch them vanish around the edge of the wall that bordered the carpark.

The police were coming, he'd seen to that, reporting the situation as active and deadly, two words he knew would get them to his location in a hurry. His priority, once he could get to him, was to check on Victor's condition. Terrified for what might happen to Rex when he reached the main road, Albert's heart almost stopped when he heard a squeal of brakes from what sounded like a large vehicle. When he also heard a dog cry out in shock, he almost abandoned the human victim to check on his canine companion.

However, he understood his duty was to the man lying on the wet tarmac so, taking his time because it's a long way to the ground when you are nearly eighty, he got on his knees and checked for a pulse.

It was there and it was strong. Victor was out cold, which begged Albert perform a basic search for a wound. Expecting to find taser wires in the man's back or a stun gun mark on his neck, Albert instead found an egg-shaped lump on Victor's skull. His attackers hadn't been precious about taking him in one piece; they'd whacked him on the head with something and knocked him out that way.

Albert almost admired the old-school brutality of it. Provided they hadn't caved his skull in, which Albert didn't think they had, Victor ought to recover and regain consciousness soon. At least that's what he told himself with optimism. Sitting back on his heels and feeling very weary, Albert heard sirens in the distance and shouted for his dog.

Rex couldn't hear his human, there was too much noise where he was as humans came from all over, stopping their cars in the middle of the road to tend to the body in the gutter. He was out of breath, panting hard despite the cool air and his soaked coat. Hans was hurt, his front left paw torn and bleeding, but his attitude had changed.

'You saved me,' he said, looking up at Rex. He was holding his front left paw in the air rather than put it down, but he knew it wasn't badly hurt. When Rex knocked him over, the sudden change in direction ripped the centre pad away from the skin along one side. It was bleeding a lot, but it didn't hurt half as much as his face. Where the human kicked him, a tooth broke, his upper canine on the right side of his face. That whole side of his head and his shoulder were one big bruise. Adrenalin had carried him through the pain, but now that they were stopped, he could appreciate just how much it hurt. 'I can't believe you did that,' Hans murmured.

Rex lowered his head so it was close to the dachshund's. 'It was that right thing to do. As was chasing and tackling the human. I was impressed. You did an amazing job of bringing one down. I wouldn't have been able to get both by myself.' Rex was being generous, he thought he probably could have taken them both, but he hadn't needed to find out and that deserved some praise. Would he have wanted to tackle a fully grown male human if he were the size of a haggis?

Hans limped forward a step on three paws. 'I'm sorry for what I said about your mother. I'm sure she never got it on with a skunk, a marmoset, and a vacuum cleaner at the same time. I was just being unkind.'

Rex lifted his head to look at what was happening a few yards away. The rain continued to fall, running off the buildings through the gutters and downpipes where it gurgled and spluttered. Sheets of it ran across the pavement which gently sloped toward the road where a stream ran along the edge to vanish into drains. Close to the nearest drain, three humans were kneeling over the broken body of a fourth. Rex didn't know who it was that he'd been chasing, only that his own human thought it a good idea.

Rex had tried to tell his human about these men while they were in Hans's house, but maybe now it would be possible to make him listen. Whatever was going on in this town had the two men he and Hans had chased at its centre. The two were reduced to one but the other had escaped. Looking down again, he asked, 'Can you walk?'

Hans licked his lips and bit his teeth together. 'I'll manage. You want to check on your human?'

'I think we should.'

But as Rex tried to set off, a police car swung into the side road they had chased the men from, cutting off their route and more police were arriving from their rear.

Rex still had his lead attached to his collar. His human had simply let it go when he told him to chase. Hans had lost his at some point complete with his collar, but the police swarmed the two dogs, and before they had a chance to realise what was going on, Hans was scooped into the air and a male police office grabbed Rex's lead and held on tight.

'Hey! What are you doing?' Rex span and pranced, trying to get free.

'I think this one is hurt,' said the cop holding Hans. The dachshund had cried out in pain when the cop grabbed him, though it could have been any one of a dozen wounds the cop touched by mistake.

Yet another voice called out to get their attention, this one farther up the side road where he had found Albert in the courtyard. Behind them in the street, paramedics forced their way through to the mess that remained of Eugene and cops attempted to clear the traffic while the rain continued to sheet from the black sky above.

Albert heard Rex coming before he saw him. Or, rather, he heard the poor cop trying to control him swearing at Rex as the headstrong oversized German Shepherd pulled the man along behind him like a kite.

He was cold now and weary, the rainwater soaking his clothes carrying his body heat away faster than he could replenish it. Albert didn't think it was cold enough out for him to need to worry about hypothermia, but his fingers were numb now and he wasn't sure he could get up. Cops arrived, followed swiftly by paramedics, everyone getting soaked as the rain refused to let up.

'Is this your dog, sir?' asked a male officer. He had hold of Rex but needed to brace and lean the other way to keep the dog in check. Rex wanted to check on his human, the ambivalence he felt toward him earlier, now far from his mind.

Wanting to give the man a break, Albert said, 'Sit, Rex.' Which the dog did automatically upon hearing the command. Doing so meant the taut lead went suddenly slack and the poor cop fell on his backside in a puddle much to the amusement of his colleagues. 'Yes, officer, this is my dog. I'm glad to see he is not hurt. Did he cause an accident?'

'The cause of the accident remains to be determined, sir.' It was a new voice that answered, but one which Albert recognised. Turning his head, he found DS Craig looking down at him. Can I ask what you are doing in a dark car park with an injured man, sir?'

He didn't get an answer, not from Albert at least because a young female paramedic, a pretty girl with short ginger hair and freckles, took a moment from assisting her colleague to get in the detective's face. 'You can ask questions later. I need to get both of my patients into the back of the ambulance and to the hospital. One has a suspected concussion and let's hope it is no worse than that, and Albert here,' she'd asked his name the moment she knelt down to check on him, 'needs to get warm before the cold becomes a problem.'

DS Craig held out his hands in a mocking gesture of surrender, making himself look the fool to Albert's mind, but he chose to answer the man's question anyway. 'I am looking into the murder of Joel Clement. Kate Harris didn't do it.' It was a bold and challenging statement, one designed to get the attention of all the police officers within earshot. Now that he had that, he continued to explain. 'The injury to Victor Harris was inflicted by two men who I interrupted in the act of kidnap. They were placing him into this van,' he pointed a wobbly finger at the non-descript white Ford Transit, 'when I chanced upon them.'

DS Craig narrowed his eyes. 'Kate Harris killed Joel Clement to get his half of the Clanger Café. It was simple greed. She has a criminal record for violent crime, plus motive and no alibi. I can assure you, sir, Kate Harris is guilty no matter what you might believe.'

Albert shook his head. The paramedics were getting ready to load Victor onto a gurney. Like Albert, he was soaked right through and would need a complete change of clothing. It would be Albert's turn next, but he wasn't done with the detective. 'You need to find out who the two men here were. They attacked Kate Harris's brother for a reason. Kidnap is not a random act, Sergeant.'

'Well one of them is currently very dead,' DS Craig replied utterly deadpan. 'The paramedics there worked on him but assure me he is not going to get better any time soon.' He was making light of the man's death. If Albert were DS Craig's superior officer, he would be tearing a strip off him right now. 'You're right though. I do need to determine who the man is. If there was indeed a second one, I shall want to know his identity too. Perhaps Mr Harris will be able to tell me who they are and why they wanted him when he regains consciousness, but my questions for you mostly revolve around whether your dog is dangerous.'

'What!' Albert's lips were going numb, but he was able to blurt his response. 'You cannot be serious!'

DS Craig's face was emotionless when he replied. 'I have blood on the street and though you tell me there were two men, I have only one, he is dead, and he has clearly been bitten by a dog if the paramedics are to be believed.'

It was Hans who bit him, Albert thought. He'd watched the two dogs until they ran out of sight and hadn't seen Rex bite either of them. He didn't say that though, he said, 'They were defending Victor Harris, the victim of an attempted kidnapping, or do you think the dogs were driving the van as part of their crime spree?'

The question drew a snigger from a couple of the cops who got a warning look from DS Craig. He brought his eyes back to Albert's. 'What then? The two men who came here to allegedly kidnap Mr Harris are the same men responsible for killing Joe Clement? Why? Are they after the top-secret clanger recipe that only two people in the world know?' Now it was his turn to make a joke, sharing it with the cops around him who took the bait and chuckled politely. 'I don't know who you are, sir, and I don't much care. Animal services are on their way to collect the dogs. They will be taken care of and if your story checks out, or can be corroborated by Mr Harris, then they will be returned to you.'

Victor was already loaded into the ambulance and now it was Albert's turn. Albert let them help him to his feet. He was cold, not injured, but far more than either thing, he was angry. The police found Albert kneeling over an injured man. Victor was unconscious, and the cops had a dead body lying in the gutter just a few yards away on the other side of the building. As the only person available to give comment, Albert could be the one responsible for it all. He doubted anyone believed that, but DS Craig sent a cop to the hospital with him anyway.

Rex couldn't work out what was going on. His human was being taken care of, it seemed; he looked cold and Rex wanted to get him back into the warm somewhere. The human holding his lead wouldn't let him get to him though and now it looked like they were taking his human somewhere. Why wasn't he going with him? He went everywhere with his human.

'Calm, Rex,' Albert called from the back of the ambulance. 'It will be okay. I'll see you soon. Go with the nice police officers and be a good dog. Okay?'

Rex didn't know what to make of it. A short while ago, he was having the best time, playing chase with the two humans. But then the air stank like blood, which he didn't like, and now they were taking his human away. Where was he going? When would he be back? Who was going to look after his human if he wasn't there to do it? It was his job.

The ambulance doors closed with a thump, and the flashing lights lit the walls of the courtyard. As it started to pull away, Rex tipped back his head and howled, a low mournful sound that made everyone in the courtyard stop and look.

Francis didn't see what happened to Eugene. He hadn't realised his partner was that close behind when he darted in front of the truck. The squeal of brakes and the thump of steel on flesh brought his head around but even then, he only got a brief impression of something flying through the air. All he knew was that it wasn't a dog.

He'd kept running, getting some distance between him and the nightmare situation in the courtyard. He'd never been to jail. He'd never even been arrested, and though he knew he was employed for criminal activities, it had never really occurred to him until this point that he might one day get caught.

It was an epiphany.

Sirens wailed behind him as he stepped into a black alleyway to catch his breath. He'd run hard enough to give himself a stitch which he rubbed at now as he tried to get his heart rate to calm down. He felt for sure the dog was going to catch him, and now he was worried it might be able to track his scent or something.

He pushed on, not wanting to stay in this town any longer than he had to and beginning to feel truly concerned about all of the mistakes he had made. His fingerprints were all over the van for a start. He suspected, when Eugene failed to answer his phone for the umpteenth time, that the thing he saw flying through the air was his partner in crime. Was he injured? Would he talk? All these questions played over and over in his mind until he stepped in front of a car and almost got run over.

The car screeched to a halt, the driver getting out despite the rain. For a second, Francis thought he was going to have to threaten the man to make him go away, but he was just showing concern. A man in his late sixties who just wanted to make sure the man he almost ran over was all right.

Seizing the opportunity presented, Francis grabbed a fistful of the man's coat and raised his fist to knock him out. The blow never landed though because the man fainted first. With a shrug, he opened the boot, shoved the limp body inside, and stole the car. He even found a surprise bonus waiting for him on the passenger's seat where the man's fish 'n' chip supper lay as yet untouched.

Happy to see Biggleswade vanish into his rear mirror as he munched on the unknown man's chips, Francis's smile soon fell when his phone rang. He didn't even need to look to know who it was calling.

'Eugene is dead,' he announced the moment the call connected.

After a brief pause, Earl Bacon's response came, 'Why would you tell me that? Have you got Mr Harris?'

Francis snorted a mad laugh. 'Have I got Mr Harris?' he repeated. 'No, I haven't, you crazy food-obsessed lunatic. Getting Victor Harris is off the menu, or you can find someone else to do the job for you. I'm not going back; the police are crawling all over Biggleswade now.'

The earl gnashed his teeth. How dare the insolent idiot defy him? 'I gave you a task to do and I expect it to be done. What excuse do you have for your failure?'

'Excuse? I dunno. The task was ridiculous? We didn't have enough time to adequately prepare? Pick one. The old man and his dog kept showing up every time we tried to grab the target.'

'What?' Did he hear that right? 'An old man and a dog? What kind of dog?'

Francis screwed his face up in the dark of the car. Why on earth was the earl asking about the dog? 'A big German Shepherd thing. Enormous beast, that's for sure.'

It couldn't be. It was just too much coincidence to be possible. 'The old man, describe him to me.'

Francis had his finger poised on the button to end the call. He wanted no further part of this madness. The money was good, but what good was it if you were dead or behind bars? Yet something in the earl's voice kept him on the line – he'd just begged Francis for information. He'd never used a pleading tone before. He just barked orders and expected them to be obeyed.

'The old man must be around eighty years old, I guess. There're only a few wisps of hair left on his head and he's got that sort of slightly hunched look like he's been standing up for a great many years and his body is starting to defy him. Oh, he's white,' Francis thought to throw in his skin colour for good measure. 'He's around six feet tall and he looks like lots of other old men.'

Earl Bacon was still struggling to believe that it could be the same man. It was one thing to get in his way in Stilton. He'd been utterly enraged at the time but had mellowed since. Pursuing one old man for revenge over the cheese was nothing but an unnecessary distraction. If it were the same man now though … well, how could it be? To interfere twice in a matter of days would suggest that he knew the earl's plan and was trying to scupper it. Why would he? What possible motivation could he have?

Gripped by paranoia, the earl found he was biting his nails, a terrible habit his father spent years scolding him for. Taking his fingers from his mouth, Earl Bacon knew he had to find out what the old man knew.

'Bring him to me,' he commanded.

'The old man?'

'Yes.'

'No. Biggleswade is too hot. You'll just have to find someone else, Your Earlness. That's enough for me. I'm out.'

The earl almost blew his top, and he was seething with fury when he switched tactic. 'I'll give you a million pounds,' he stated quietly, confident it would change his employee's attitude.

Francis almost crashed the car. 'A million!'

'Yes.' Earl Bacon had no interest in money, only what it could be used for. He couldn't possibly spend what he had and there was no point in hanging on to it, what worth would silly bits of paper have once the world ended? He could give it all to Francis if that were what it took to make sure he could be safe and secure in his bunker when the end came. 'A million. I will transfer half of it now and the rest when you deliver Mr Harris and the old man to me.'

'You want the dog too?' Francis asked.

Shaking his head at the man's stupidity, the earl asked, 'What purpose could I possibly have for the dog? Kill it if it gets in your way. Just get me that old man. I need him alive. He has questions to answer.'

Francis sucked air between his teeth. Everything in his head was telling him to put the accelerator down and keep driving until he ran out of land and then cross whichever sea he had come to. A million pounds was a lot of money though, and with it, escape would be so much easier. He knew the earl had it. Chances were, if he checked his account now, the half up front would already be in there.

'Okay,' he said, with some resignation, slowing the car as he started to look for a place to turn. He was going back to Biggleswade, and now, by himself, he had two men to kidnap.

Unhappy when they took his human away and even more so when they corralled him into a cage inside a van, Rex felt genuine relief to have Hans with him. The sausage dog went into the cage next to his, lowered gently onto a blanket by the lady holding him. She spoke soothingly to both dogs, promising them a comfortable place to sleep, food, water, a check-up, which Rex wasn't too sure about – it sounded like it might involve a thermometer – and all the attention they deserved.

The van ride hadn't been a long one, and true to her word, the lady had snacks in her hand when they arrived wherever they were. The snacks proved to be a lure to get him inside the building – Hans got carried – where they then wanted to bath him. He was already soaked, his fur stuck to his body to make him look fifty percent smaller than usual so what on Earth did they want to bath him for?

'I don't need a bath!' Rex barked, bucking against the lead as the man holding him tried to drag him toward the obvious doggy shower facility.

'Just a quick splash and tickle,' the man assured Rex. 'You're a bit stinky and there is mud in your coat, big fella.'

Rex bucked again, this time slipping his collar with a triumphant bark, 'Not a chance, puny human! I am dog and shall outwit you!'

He pranced away, but a heavenly scent caught his nose and made him stop.

From somewhere out of sight, Hans' voice drifted out, 'What is that? It smells amazing!'

Rex's nose was in the air. He was going to get caught by the man again, but he couldn't help himself; he had to know where the smell was coming from. It smelled like all the best bits of meat all condensed down into one nose-curling odour.

'Want some?' asked the man.

Rex's eyes popped out like they were on stalks. The man he'd just given the slip wasn't chasing him and trying to wrestle him back into the shower, he was offering Rex something that was causing long ribbons of drool to fall from his jowls.

The man backed away and Rex followed. Floating on a cushion of the unbelievable smell, Rex was powerless to stop his legs walking all the way into the shower. The man kept the jar just out of reach; Rex would need to jump into the air to get to it, but the human was saying he could have it.

As they came into the shower, the man stuck his hand into the jar, scooping a big blob of the dark sticky mass before smearing it onto the tile at Rex's nose height.

Rex fell upon it, licking at the blob with his rough tongue. Behind his ears something was happening, but he wasn't really aware of it, whatever it was.

Chuckling to himself as he started to work shampoo into the big dog's coat, the man said, 'The old Bovril trick. It gets them every time.'

Albert awoke disorientated and a little confused, staring at the unfamiliar room for a second before his brain caught up with him. He was in hospital, of course. Memories of the previous evening flooded back and along with them, concern for Rex, Victor, and Hans the sausage dog in that order. Animal services would take care of Rex, he was confident of that, but how would Rex react to being taken away by people he didn't know? He could be so headstrong when he wanted to be.

Sitting up in bed, Albert could see that he was in a room of four beds. Three were occupied, only the one opposite his feet was empty and the sleeping form diagonally opposite was Victor. Albert could see his face; the colour in it was a healthy shade, not deathly pallid, and though he was sleeping, he wasn't hooked up to a bank of machines to monitor his vital signs.

Turning his head toward the window, Albert found his clothes from the previous day neatly folded in a pile on a chair. Someone had cleaned, dried, and ironed them. His shoes even looked to have been polished.

There appeared to be no hospital staff around and no noise coming from outside of the room to indicate there were people there. 'Do I press the call button?' he asked himself. Not getting an answer, he decided to get himself dressed instead because he always felt naked and exposed in hospital gowns. He would be happier meeting people if he were dressed in his own clothes.

Gently tugging the curtains around his bed until he was shut off from view, Albert doffed the gown and that was when he found he was wearing hospital issue underpants. That meant someone had put them on him. No doubt his were soaked through, but he couldn't help feeling a cringe as he pictured a pretty young nurse pulling down his undergarments.

With a sigh, he dropped the white cotton shorts and picked up his own. Of course, that was when the nurse on her rounds pulled back the curtain to see inside.

Albert heard the curtain open and span around, his blue paisley underpants in his hands and his meat and two veg on display.

'Good morning,' she trumpeted.

'Arrrgh!' he screamed.

Unperturbed by his terrified yell, the nurse advanced, dropping her clipboard on the bed. 'Would you like a hand to get dressed, dear?' She was coming forward with her hands out to take his underwear.

She was a short woman with wide hips and large round glasses that made her eyes look bulbous. In her late thirties, Albert felt sure she would claim to have seen it all before and no doubt she had, but now he couldn't decide whether he wanted to use the paisley shorts to cover himself, or whip them around behind his back so that she couldn't get to them.

'I can manage,' he stammered.

'It's okay to get a little help, love. We all get old.' She was still coming forward, her hands at his groin height and reaching forward. If he pulled the shorts away now, she might grab something else.

'Did I hear a scream?' asked another nurse, pushing the curtain aside as she too came to help. 'Is everything all right?'

Her colleague turned her head to reply. 'The poor dear just needs a little help getting dressed.'

Nurse number two, a slightly younger and much slimmer version of nurse one, gave Albert a sweet, encouraging smile. 'Hi,' she said. 'This won't take us a moment. Veronica and I do this every day. We'll get you dressed and then we'll sort you out a nice bit of breakfast.'

Now Albert had two women advancing on him, and he was still naked. If they would just turn around or go away, he could get some clothing on his skin and regain his dignity. All he could manage to do was back away with his undershorts held firmly to his groin. 'I don't need any help,' he stated firmly.

Unbelievably, the curtain twitched again as yet another nurse came through it. This one looked to be at least ten years older and wore a darker blue uniform. Her stern, no-nonsense expression made Albert think she had to be the matron.

'What's going on here?' she barked though Albert wasn't sure if the question was aimed at him or the nurses.

'We're just giving Mr Smith a hand to get dressed,' said nurse two. 'He's a little shy, I think.'

'No, I don't ...' Albert managed before the matron cut him off, uninterested in what he might have to say.

'Hurry up about it then,' she barked at the nurses. 'The police are here to see him.'

Just about ready to abandon being polite, Albert's eye flared even wider when the curtain shifted yet again, and DS Craig came through the gap. Worse yet, he had a young female officer with him, and it was her reaction that tipped Albert over the edge.

The girl spotted Albert, glanced down to his groin, and back up but by then she was looking away and trying to stifle a laugh.

Albert threw his shorts on the bed, letting his tackle swing free. 'Get out!' he roared. 'Every last one of you. I have been dressing myself since my age was in single figures and I am not so old that I can no longer manage.'

His outburst made the two nurses, who were closest to him, back away a pace. Albert locked eyes with DS Craig who needed no further encouragement. He swivelled on the spot, and shoving the young female officer ahead of him, he beat a hasty retreat.

Nurse one tugged the curtain back in place with a final, 'Just call if you do need a hand with buttons or anything,' and finally Albert was alone. He dressed swiftly, determined to prove a point, but in doing so, he discovered his body had developed a few aches. His hips and knees for a start which he attributed to all the walking he had done over the last two days. In Bakewell and Stilton, he'd gone around in a car a lot of the time and in Melton Mowbray, the distances he'd needed to cover were generally not that great. Over the last two days in Biggleswade, he'd challenged himself and the aches he now felt were the penalty. His lower back was stiff too, and he resigned himself to taking it a little easier.

Once his sweater was in place, and his shoes were tied with neat reef knots, he pulled the curtain open and stepped through it to reveal himself.

'Your sweater's on inside out,' commented DS Craig who was leaning against the wall half in and half out of the doorway.

Looking down to confirm he wasn't lying, Albert swore and muttered, then took it off, reversed it and tried again. He'd been awake for thirty minutes and it already felt it was going to be one of those days.

'Where is my dog?' Albert demanded to know.

DS Craig pushed himself off the wall but didn't answer straight away. He eyed Albert steadily for a second. 'I've arranged to have him brought to the station. I need to take a statement from you, and I have a number of questions as you might imagine.'

Albert was pleased to hear they were bringing Rex to him, but he wasn't ready to play ball with the DS just yet; he was still sore about his treatment last night. Rather than thank him, Albert turned his attention toward Victor.

'How is he, do you know?' he asked the detective.

DS Craig moved into the room, coming to stand beside Albert at the foot of Victor's bed. 'I'm told he has no lasting injuries, just a nasty contusion on his head. They performed a scan – I don't remember what the right word for it is – on his head last night. They assured me his brain is fine. Beyond that I don't know much, other than that he regained consciousness an hour after they brought him in here and he is sleeping now. I want to interview him too, but they were adamant that I not wake him. We should probably move away, in fact.'

Thirty years ago, Albert would have just woken the man if he was in the middle of a murder enquiry and had questions to ask, but then he didn't live in a small rural community where the matron would remember his disobedience and might punish him for it next time.

As they both left the room, the matron appeared, blocking their path. 'Mr Smith you are not yet discharged,' she pointed out in a manner that made it clear she expected him to return to his room and wait until he was.

Albert had no time for that but recognised the service her staff had provided. 'Please pass on my thanks to your colleagues. Most especially to whoever took care of my clothes. I'm afraid I must go now. People are waiting for me and there is a killer to catch.'

His statement made DS Craig's head whip around to look at him, but the detective kept quiet.

'But you are not discharged,' the matron complained when Albert neatly sidestepped her.

DS Craig went with him, turning around to walk backwards so he could talk to the matron. 'You'll be sure to let me know when Mr Harris is awake, yes?'

Unused to being disobeyed, the matron folded her arms and glared until they were out of sight.

Going out of the double doors to the carpark, DS Craig said, 'I looked you up. You had quite the career.'

'What made you do that?' asked Albert.

DS Craig chuckled. 'I got a call from a detective superintendent called Gary Smith. He warned me that you were in town and that we might cross paths. He said you have a knack for finding trouble.' Albert frowned but didn't say anything which prompted DS Craig to say more. 'I should probably let you know that we found Joel Clement's prints inside the Ford Transit van. And his blood and pieces of hair.'

This was news, and it was welcome news at that. The detective lifted his right arm, plipping the button on a set of keys to open a silver Ford Mondeo. Pausing before he opened the passenger door to get in, Albert said, 'You have released Kate Harris then?'

DS Craig had his door open but stopped himself from getting in when he heard the surprising question. 'Why ever would I do that?'

Albert's eyes flared. 'Why? Because he was kidnapped by the two men with the van. One of them is dead; you found him in the street, I understand. The other is on the run if he has any sense. Those two are responsible for snatching Joel Clement and taking him to Wales. They killed him, or they are involved. I won't claim to know what is going on, but you must be questioning how Kate Harris can possibly be involved.'

DS Craig shook his head. 'Not at all. I had been wondering how she managed to get him to Wales. Did she trick him into the trip? Did she get him into her car and then knock him out? The two accomplices provide the missing elements of her crime. You were a police officer for many years, Mr Smith, you must know that statistically, most crimes are driven by financial greed and those that aren't mostly revolve around sex.'

Albert did know that. He was a person who, when serving, reminded other officers of that fact on a regular basis. Despite that, he didn't think it was the case this time. There was something else going on here. 'How do you explain them coming back for Victor Harris then? If Kate Harris is the master criminal with two henchmen in her service, what was her motivation for the kidnap of her brother?' Albert watched as the question finally made the detective sergeant pause: he hadn't considered that.

Feeling like he'd finally made a point that might stick, Albert slid inside the detective's unmarked police car. 'Take me to my dog, please.'

DS Craig pulled his car into the small carpark behind the station just as the animal services van arrived. Albert had seen it coming down the road toward them from the opposite direction and hoped it would prove to have Rex inside.

It did, the dog bouncing on all four paws as the handler tried to keep him calm.

'Hey, human!' barked Rex, wagging his tail excitedly.

'What happened to his coat?' asked Albert, closing the distance between them so he could fuss his dog. 'He looks kind of … poofey,' he searched for the right word.

The handler, a heavyset Asian man in his forties wearing thick-rimmed black glasses seemed only too happy to hand Rex's lead over. 'There's no doubt you're his owner. The fur is like that because we used the hair dryer to get the water out of his coat. On some dogs it adds a lot of volume,' he explained.

He turned to close the rear doors of the van or, at least, that's what Albert thought he was doing, but the man bent down and reached inside instead. When he straightened once more, he had Hans in his arms. 'I believe this one is yours too.'

The man was pushing Hans in his direction. The smaller dog had a big blue bandage around his front left paw. Albert didn't know what had happened to him; he hadn't seen the injury last night. He didn't ask about it though, he said, 'Hans is not my dog.'

The animal services man looked surprised, and also confused as to what he should do now.

130

DS Craig came to the rescue, holding out his arms for the dog. 'It belongs to the victim of an attack last night. I'll see he is delivered to the correct person.'

Satisfied that he'd done his duty, the animal services man closed his van and left. No sooner did the car start to pull away, than DS Craig handed Albert the sausage dog. 'I'm not a dog person, Mr Smith and you clearly are. Would you mind looking after him until we are done?' He didn't wait for an answer, he simply thrust Hans into Albert's arms and walked toward a door in the back of the police station.

Rex and Albert were back together, but now they had an unexpected extra.

'This is fun,' said Hans. 'What are we doing now?'

Frowning, Albert tottered after the detective who was now holding the door open and waiting to go inside. Led to an office that doubled as an interview room, Albert told Rex to lie down but kept Hans on his lap. He'd seen how the dogs were when together yesterday and when the dachshund tried to get to the floor, Albert carefully plopped him onto his feet well away from Rex. However, to Albert's amazement, the smaller dog crossed the room to curl up touching the large German Shepherd. It made a small snort of laughter escape his mouth just as DS Craig came back into the room with two mugs of tea.

'Now then, sir,' DS Craig settled into the chair opposite Albert, 'I would like a blow by blow account of last night, please, and don't spare the detail.'

Albert walked the detective through all that had happened but went back to the point where DS Craig entered his story: in the Clanger Café two days ago when he arrested Kate Harris. He told DS Craig about how he came to be involved, about going to Kate's house, but left out the part about April and the suspicious missing money. When he finished, he asked, 'You still think Kate Harris did it?'

DS Craig was looking down at the notes he'd taken. The interview was recorded, of course, but he liked to keep pertinent points to hand. He heard Albert's question but didn't look up straight away because the appearance of the two men was troubling him. Once he was finished with Mr Smith, he was going to HMP Bedford prison to interview Kate Harris. He liked his post in Biggleswade; he got to be the boss here with only a semi-regular visit from the superintendent from Bedford. All that could change if he had too many bodies cluttering up the morgue. Joel Clement might not have been killed here but the crime was still his to investigate and now he had an unknown man in the morgue; a man who had been involved in a crime immediately before his death. That he carried no identification and the van they used was equally bereft of clues to his identify made him question what he might have uncovered.

DS Craig had thought the case sewn up when he took Kate Harris into custody. Now he wasn't so sure. Looking up finally, he said, 'Yes, I do. I think she planned the murder meticulously, setting it up years in advance when she met Joel Clement and saw an opportunity. On Saturday night, she arrived home, whacked her boyfriend over the head and dragged him out to the van where her two accomplices were waiting. Either they killed him, or she did, but his body went the rest of the way to Wales in the van and was dumped at the side of the road. She waited two days and made a big show of trying to find Joel Clement herself before finally reporting him to the police as a missing person. She thought she had got away clean, but I guess her brother found out or worked it out because she sent the two men to silence him.'

Albert let his head drop forward so he was looking at the mismatched carpet tile. There was no point in presenting any further argument.

132

DS Craig gathered his things together, closed his notebook and put his pen back into his jacket inner pocket. 'Thank you for your statement regarding the incident last night. If you'll excuse me, I need to travel to HMP Bedford now; Miss Harris has some more questions to answer. I suggest you drop your interest in this case, sir. Kate Harris is a cold-blooded killer and she has you wrapped around her little finger. While Joel Clement's body was slowly going cold on Saturday night, she was most likely eating her dinner and enjoying a bottle of wine. I'll have one of my constables escort you out, sir.'

DS Craig left the room, walking away without another word. Albert couldn't decide if he thought the man incompetent or if he might read the clues the same way if he were leading the investigation. The case against Kate was a good one.

Alone in the room, Albert thought some more about what he still needed to do today. Far from dropping his interest, it was now as piqued as it could be. More certain than ever that DS Craig was trying to make the pieces fit and fooling himself that they did, Albert knew he might be the only person between Kate Harris and a long, yet undeserved, jail sentence.

Pushing against weary knees to get back onto his feet, Albert knew what he was going to do next.

Side-tracked

Albert was on his way to breakfast. He wanted to continue to pursue the case: he felt like he had no choice now, but he also needed to get some food and take it easier today. His plan was to visit the Clanger Café and park himself there for a short while.

However, fate intervened, and he only got as far as the front desk of the police station. A morose looking man in his sixties was waiting there for someone to deal with him but at the same time – proving men can easily multi-task – he was getting an ear bashing from his wife. It had to be the man's wife, Albert surmised, because no one else would ever talk so harshly to a person.

Her issue appeared to be that she didn't believe there was any reason for her husband to be wasting her time or that of the police with some made up story about a man kidnapping him.

'But, love, there was a man. He made me get in the boot of the car.' In truth he'd woken in the boot of the car but didn't want to admit that he'd fainted when he thought he was going to get thumped.

'Oh, stop it, Eric!' his wife snapped in reply. 'Just admit you went to the pub and ate all the chips. This charade has gone on long enough.'

'But I didn't go to the pub, love,' the man complained. He was facing the counter, rather than his wife, eyes forward and looking meek. He was short at maybe five and a half feet and his wife was taller by a couple of inches plus a good deal bigger in every direction. Albert had the immediate impression the woman had been verbally bullying the man for many decades. 'I need to report this for insurance purposes if nothing else.'

'Oh, yes,' she replied, clearly not believing a word, 'because you pranged the car and now won't admit it.' The argument continued unabated as the young constable leading Albert from the police station got to the door that led back into reception.

At the front desk, the duty officer was on the phone and trying to wrap the call up so he could deal with the annoying couple. It was of no interest to Albert whose thoughts were only of breakfast and a nice pot of tea. He had Rex leading the way and Hans tucked under his left arm, but Rex stopped walking, suddenly spinning around to sniff the man at the desk.

'He knows the human I chased last night!' woofed Rex, instantly animated and excited. He sniffed along the man's jacket, sucking in a deep noseful of the familiar scent.

'Is it him?' growled Hans.

Rex sniffed deeply, but his presence was making the couple uncomfortable. 'What is this?' asked the woman.

Rex barked, the loud and sudden noise making the woman jump backward in fright whereupon she let out a small scream. 'Arrrgh! There's a mad dog!'

'Rex, sit,' ordered Albert, his well-trained dog obeying. Albert was learning to observe his dog's behaviour and there was definitely something about what he was seeing. His dog could smell something on the man that made him agitated. 'Did I hear you say you were kidnapped last night?'

The woman, calm again now that the dog was under control, rolled her eyes. 'We're perfectly fine, thank you. There's no need to get involved. Eric is going to lie to the police to cover up going to the pub and driving home drunk because he ate my supper and crashed the car.'

The duty officer on the front desk finally finished his phone call. 'Now then, sir,' he gave Eric his undivided attention. 'What can I help you with this morning?'

Caught for a second, his attention split between the officer, his wife, and an old man who actually seemed to believe what he had to say, Eric decided he needed to answer the officer first. 'I stopped to help a man last night after I almost ran him over. He forced me into the boot of my car and took it.'

'No, he didn't!' snapped his wife. 'That's enough now, Eric.'

The duty officer watched the interplay with disinterest, but a crime had been reported and he was duty bound to log it.

'I would have come in last night,' Eric whined, 'but my wife wouldn't hear of it.'

'That's because it is stupid,' she growled at the back of his head. A small tick next to Eric's eye began to twitch.

'What did he look like?' asked Albert, splitting the man's attention again.

The duty officer looked up from his computer. 'If you don't mind, sir,' he used his official cop voice which might have worked on most people but had no impact on Albert at all.

Albert was curious to hear one piece of information. 'Was he a tall, muscular man wearing combat fatigues?'

Eric eyes flared wide. 'Yeah!'

'Short light brown hair, yes?' Albert sought to confirm.

'Yes!' Eric had turned himself to face the older man.

Albert swung his face and eyes to look at the duty officer. 'You may wish to get DS Craig to speak with this gentleman, I believe he met with the man responsible for the attempted kidnapping of Victor Harris last night.' Frowning as the next question presented itself, Albert looked at Eric again. 'How did you escape?'

Stood just behind Eric, and tall enough to look over his head, his wife sighed in an exasperated way. 'He didn't escape! He's making the whole thing up.'

The tic on Eric's face twitched again, and to Albert, it was the warning sign of a volcano about to erupt. Before the man could reach that point, Albert prompted a reply. 'You got away. Did he not close the boot correctly?'

Eric shrugged. 'I think he forgot about me. I was in the car for a while. He started driving and I think we left town because all the background noise went away. Then I could hear him talking on the phone but couldn't make out what he was saying. There were two voices: his and someone very posh-sounding. When the phone call ended, he must have turned the car around. I thought that was what he did, but when the engine went off again, he got out, and after a minute or so, I found the release button to fold the back seat down. He was nowhere in sight and the keys were still in the ignition.'

Eric looked relieved to have finally told the story to someone who believed him. The duty officer had made the call to get DS Craig, but as Albert heard footsteps coming their way from behind the reception desk, the woman grabbed Eric's arm and tried to pull him away.

'That's it! I'm not listening to anymore of this rubbish! You are coming home right this minute, Eric Simpson.' She had hold of the sleeve of his

137

coat and was already starting to drag him toward the door as if he were a naughty child being taken home by an enraged mother.

The volcano blew it's top. Albert had to wonder how long the pressure inside had been building because the torrent of expletives erupting from the small man's mouth was quite impressive. Giving Albert the impression it was the first time Eric had ever stood up to her, he listened as the downtrodden husband raged and spat and cursed at his wife for a full minute.

DS Craig arrived behind the front desk, ready to ask a question but forced into silence by the one-sided verbal onslaught. Albert glanced his way in time to see his eyes as wide as the duty officer's.

With a final threat of divorce if she so much as ever questioned him again, Eric told her to, 'Go and wait in the car.'

It was then that Albert intervened. 'No! Not the car.' Swinging his attention to DS Craig's curious face, Albert said, 'I think the man who escaped last night has left his prints all over this gentleman's car.'

Detective Sergeant Craig scratched his head. It had been an odd couple of days. The last recorded murder in Biggleswade was twenty-seven years ago. He was more used to dealing with kids stealing things from the local supermarket. Occasionally he had a domestic violence case to deal with and once, he even had a fraud case that ended in a stabbing. He was feeling quite out of his depth, not that he would admit it to anyone, but he couldn't ignore that the old man might be right and needed to show everyone that he was not only in charge, but on top of what was happening.

'Impound the car,' he instructed the officer standing two feet from him. 'Get the crime scene team back here.' Then to Eric, he said, 'I think, sir, that I had better take a statement from you.'

138

Rex watched the man who smelled of the human he chased be taken through a door, his bewildered-looking, and suddenly silent, wife trailing along in his wake. He got another sniff as he passed in front of Rex's nose, just to double confirm what he already knew, but what now? Where was the human he chased?

Fatal Error

Arriving back in Biggleswade, Francis had promptly ditched the car in a side street and ambled away trying to look innocent. He couldn't return to the café or its vicinity because the risk he would be recognised was too great. In fact, he considered the entire town and its surrounding area to be a hot spot he ought to be avoiding. The old man had seen him, as had Victor Harris. Eugene was dead and though Francis didn't think they could easily trace his body, he was confident they would work out who Eugene was soon enough, and that might lead them to him.

He needed to get out of Biggleswade, but he couldn't do that until the job was finished. It was a paradox. To limit the risk of being identified, he needed a change of clothes to help him alter his appearance. He had more clothes with him, but they were all derivations of his current outfit. Then, rolling his eyes at his own stupidity, he remembered Eugene's clothes. They were about the same size. If the police were looking for a man in combat fatigues, they wouldn't look twice at him in a smart jacket and tie. Maybe Eugene wasn't as dumb as Francis always assumed.

It was only an hour after ditching the car that he remembered he'd left the owner in the boot. He ran back, thinking he would just have to kill him and leave the body to be found but, of course, the car was long gone.

Francis cursed himself, gritting his teeth and swearing at the sky, small gods, and anyone who would listen. There was no one in ear shot, of course, he wasn't that stupid, but now he truly felt like a man with a target on his back. He spent the night in the lockup he and Eugene had been using since they arrived in town. They'd found an empty place and broken in when they first arrived, using it to hide the van and all their equipment. It meant they had a very basic standard of living when they could be in a nice bed and breakfast, but the practice limited how many people they came into contact with and gave them somewhere secret from which to operate.

He wasn't excited about getting started today. Truthfully, he was dreading what the day might bring, but with the promise of more money than he would ever earn by any other method, Francis closed the lockup door behind him, and set out to earn a million pounds.

Victor Harris hadn't seen his face, that much he was sure of and for once letting Eugene do the talking had played to his advantage. The old man might have seen him, but he was just going to have to work with what he had. Best to get Victor first and he was fairly sure he knew where to find him.

As a wicked idea sparked into life, he allowed himself a small smile. Oh, yes. He could pull this off. He always knew he was the brains of the outfit, and now he got to prove it. Speed would be necessary; a vital factor, in fact, but if luck stayed with him, he would be out of Biggleswade by lunchtime with both men safely in his care. He needed to visit a hardware store for supplies and clothes. First things first though, he needed to steal a taxi.

Observation

Albert's stomach had been rumbling since he left hospital. He could have eaten there but the option to escape with DS Craig proved too tempting. Plus, how good could hospital breakfast be? Albert considered that he had too few years left to waste days eating bad food.

Somehow, he'd ended up with an extra dog. When DS Craig left Hans with him, Albert almost protested; the dog wasn't his responsibility, but before the words could form on his lips, he wondered if perhaps the little

Dachshund might prove useful. Either way, he was back at the Clanger Café.

Being sensibly diversified, the Clanger café specialised in their namesake dish, but served other things, and that included breakfast.

'Did they feed you?' Albert asked Rex and Hans at the door to the café.

Both dogs looked up with excited faces. Albert knew he hadn't given Rex dinner last night or breakfast this morning, and though he felt sure the animal services people would have ensured both dogs were given a nutritionally balanced meal at least once while they had them, he needed to be sure they were not going hungry.

The bell jingled above his head on the way in, making the staff behind the counter lift their heads in an automatic reaction they must repeat hundreds of times a day. Carrying Hans under his left arm – the dog became heavy after a while and had been swapped from arm to arm – Albert waved with his right. It would be wrong to say the staff knew him, but they would recognise his face from the showdown with April yesterday.

There were two women working the front counter, both looked up as he came in, but it was the one to his right behind the cash register who spoke. 'Is that Hans?' she asked, looking at the dog under his left arm.

Albert flipped his eyebrows. 'Yes, I seem to be surrogate dog owner today. I take it you have heard from Victor,' asked Albert, stepping up to the counter so they could talk without speaking rudely over the heads of the customers. Once there, he could read their name badges. The lady behind the cash register was Rita and the other lady's name was Meredith.

His question brought a look of concern from both women. 'Oh, yes,' said the talkative one. 'The police had questions for us last night. They tracked half of us to the pub on Grand Lane so we knew all about it not long after it happened.'

'It's just shocking,' said her colleague. 'Who would believe it? First Mr Clement and now Victor. Who's going to be next?'

It was a good question, but to answer it, he would first have to work out why on Earth either man had been targeted, and that was his biggest challenge. Other customers were coming through the door after him, so he swiftly changed the subject to the one which he wanted to ask. 'Is April here?' he asked, a half humorous, half serious grimace on his face.

His question got a smirk from the two women working the counter and a baker bringing goods through from the kitchen.

'No one's seen or heard from her since yesterday,' said the woman behind the cash register.

'That's not quite right,' argued her female colleague. 'Young Shannon heard from her all right.'

'What do you mean?' Albert wanted to know.

The woman behind the cash register, Rita, a lady in her forties with short curly hair held in a net and not one jot of makeup, sighed. 'She called in sick today. Shannon that is, not April. The rumour is that April banned her from coming to work until the situation with her managing the place is resolved. She's always been a bully, that April.'

'Why would Shannon obey her?' Albert wanted to know.

'April is her great aunt,' replied Rita, then bit her lip. 'Have I got that right? April is Shannon's grandmother's sister.'

Albert did the genealogy math in his head. 'Yes, that's right – great aunt. But she has a big enough hold over Shannon to stop her coming to work?'

Rita nodded. Meredith moved away to serve another customer, but Albert managed to hold Rita's attention just a little longer because this line of enquiry was interesting. It was all about the dynamics of the workplace and there had to be something in the background to explain what was going on. 'Why has April been tolerated for so long if she is such a bully?'

Rita glanced left and right as if worried she might be overheard, then leaned forward to tell him, 'The rumour is that she had dirt on the previous owner. April has been working here since the seventies. Of course, when Mr Clement bought the place ten years ago, he didn't know what she was like or he would have got shot of her straight away. Now it's a little late to fire her unless someone could prove she was doing something worthy of being fired. She'll argue that trying to take over was in the best interest of the business.'

Albert wasn't sure what to make of that and he was beginning to hold up the queue of people wanting to place an order or pay for goods from the display cabinet. He asked for a breakfast plate and a pot of tea for himself, plus a clanger to share between the two dogs. Task complete, he retired to a table in the corner where he could rest and watch.

Using his time wisely, Albert placed a call to Victor. He would either be awake, and able to answer, or still asleep, in which case Albert believed his phone would most likely be switched to silent and would therefore not disturb him.

It rang only once before Victor's voice echoed in Albert's ear. 'Is that you, Albert?'

'Good morning, Victor. How are you feeling?'

'I'm told I have you to thank for being able to feel anything. You and Rex, I guess. Did you really fight off the two men who attacked me?' Victor's voice carried a sense of disbelief, as well it should if he thought Albert had given the two miscreants what for.

Albert snorted a small laugh through his nose. 'Rex and Hans saw them off. I hid around the corner and called the police.'

'And one of them was killed when he ran into traffic. Is that right?' Victor asked.

Albert spent a minute regaling the baker with the story from his viewpoint. When he was done, he asked. 'Did they give you any indication why they wanted you?' This was the key question so far as Albert was concerned. Why on Earth would anyone want to kidnap a baker from Biggleswade? The answer had to be the key to the whole escapade and the reason why Joel Clement was dead. Was the owner mixed up in drugs? Did he borrow money from the mob to buy the café in the first place?

Victor's reply told him nothing. 'The one who spoke asked if I knew how to make a clanger. He made me promise that I could bake and had me list the ingredients and tell him how to make one. There were two of them, but I only ever saw that one. The other chap was positioned behind me the whole time and when they were satisfied that I could make a clanger, he hit me over the head from behind. I didn't see it coming, but I have quite a dent in my skull now.

They wanted him because he could cook? It beggared belief. 'Did they say anything else?' Albert begged, wondering if the blow to his head might have scrambled Victor's brain.

145

'No, that was it. Can I make a clanger? It made me wonder if they were the same people who took Joel. He couldn't cook at all.'

Of course, Victor wouldn't yet know the police had found Joel's fingerprints and DNA in the van. Albert's thoughts were drifting though, what if they had taken Joel assuming he could bake. He was the owner after all. It could then follow that he proved of no use and they killed him before returning to get someone who could bake.

Proved of no use. The sentence echoed in his head and produced a new question: of no use for what?

'Albert are you still there?' asked Victor when the silence stretched out far enough.

'Yes, Victor, sorry,' he apologised. 'Are you aware of anyone interested in starting a rival clanger company or of any reason why someone might want to know how to bake a perfect clanger?'

'A rival clanger firm? I hardly think so. There isn't enough demand for them. It's been in decline for years. There used to be dozens of places making and selling them right across the county a few decades ago. Now there is just us. The original and best,' he boasted proudly.

Across the café, Albert could see Meredith approaching with a tray. Steam rose from his breakfast and from the spout of the small pot of tea. It made his stomach gurgle with anticipation. He needed to wrap up the call now, but he wasn't quite out of questions.

'Have the police seen you yet?'

'No. Will they come here? I'd really rather leave if I'm allowed.'

Albert didn't know the answer to that particular question though he felt sure DS Craig had said something about it earlier. Worried, not for the

146

first time, that his memory was getting spotty, Albert said, 'I know they will want a statement and will have a list of questions to ask you. You could go to them instead of waiting. The sooner DS Craig can corroborate what he's been told with your version of events, the sooner he can get on with tracking down the man who got away. I think this may be the key to getting your sister released.'

'Well, that would be good,' Victor agreed. 'I'll probably do that.'

His breakfast was six feet away and closing. 'I must go, Victor. I am in your café about to enjoy some breakfast. Let me know when you are done with the police.'

'You're at the café?' Victor expressed his surprise. 'Is everything okay there? I mean, they are a few hands short now without Kate or me or … did April come in today do you know?'

The breakfast tray was set on his table so that Meredith could set out his plates and arrange his pot of tea. He ignored his phone so he could thank her and politely pay attention while she served. Only when she turned away did he answer Victor's question, 'No, she is absent, as is her grandniece, Shannon.'

'Shannon's not there?' questioned Victor. 'That is surprising.'

'Is it?' asked Albert. 'I got the impression April rules her life.'

Victor couldn't argue with that. 'I guess she does, but even so, poor Shannon has a baby and is flat broke more often than not. I'm not sure how she gets by on what she get's paid working part-time hours so taking time off makes no sense.'

The statement startled Albert. Or rather, the realisation that followed it did. He ended the call quickly thereafter, excusing himself so his long-awaited breakfast wouldn't go cold, but as he tucked into a juicy piece of sausage, he wondered if he'd just been given the answer to another small part of the mess.

His breakfast was sumptuous, just as expected, and a heaping plateful it was too. Beneath the table, Rex and Hans licked their lips and rejoiced in getting a second breakfast; a rare event if ever there was one. The animal services people had been kind to them, fussing them and making sure they were clean and dry. They tended to Hans' injured paw but the kibble they served left a lot to be desired. Not that it was inedible, it just wasn't very tasty. They ate it because it was food, but to get a tasty treat split sixty: forty in Rex's favour by his human was something neither dog had expected.

Hans saw that he got the smaller piece, but he didn't make a snarky comment which he would have to any other dog. His piece was more than big enough to fill his belly. 'That was good,' he mumbled around a satisfied burp.

Rex licked the carpet to get the last few crumbs. 'It sure was. Yet, I cannot help thinking that we ought to be out trying to catch the man from last night.'

Hans frowned. 'I thought your human said he would be miles away by now.'

Rex thought about that. 'He did, but you and I both smelled him on the man at the police station. If I understood him correctly, the man is still here.'

Above the table, Albert was thinking the same thing, but his thoughts were a little more complicated than the dogs'. His breakfast plate was empty, pushed aside so he could bring his teacup to rest between his hands. None of it made sense. That was what bothered him more than anything. If they were truly trying to kidnap Victor because he could bake

149

a clanger, then it was the strangest motive for a crime he had ever heard of. What was worse though was that the man who escaped, seemed to have found a way to evade the police and leave Biggleswade, only to return here almost immediately. Then, in a sloppy way if he didn't want to get caught, he let Eric Simpson live. What could possibly motivate him to come back to the very place where the police were looking for him?

Albert sipped his tea and pondered that question.

'The police sent a taxi for you, Mr Harris,' said the nurse.

Victor had been allowed just enough painkillers to make his headache recede into the background but not enough to make it go away. The doctor seemed unreasonably concerned that Victor might develop a painkiller addiction. Personally, he doubted that would happen and couldn't work out where he would be able to obtain such strong painkillers anyway. Nevertheless, he was dressed, discharged and ready to go. A Detective Sergeant called Craig had left a message with the nurses' station to call him when Victor was awake, but before they had the chance to call, a taxi driver arrived to collect him.

'I guess they arranged for someone else to take my statement,' he commented to the nurse.

'Do you have everything you came in with?' she asked, checking about his bed to make sure the outgoing patient didn't need to make a return trip.

Victor chuckled. 'I was unconscious when I arrived. I'm not sure what I came in with.' Switching to serious when she gave him a puzzled look, he said, 'I'm sure I haven't left anything behind. I have my wallet, phone, and house keys.'

She escorted him back to the nurses' station where the taxi driver stood reading a poster and looking bored.

'This is Mr Harris?' the man sought to confirm.

Though the man hadn't addressed him, Victor extended his hand. 'Pleased to meet you.' There was something familiar about the man, but he couldn't put his finger on why. He saw so many people coming in and out of the café that he was probably just another customer.

The taxi driver, a large man wearing a casual but smart jacket – one too smart for the average taxi driver - shook his hand lightly and began meandering back toward the entrance. 'I got a spot right out front,' he said over his shoulder.

'Did they say who I need to speak to when I get there?' Victor asked.

The man shrugged, his over-developed trapezius muscles hunching up and then down again. 'The woman at the cab firm tells me where to go and who to collect.' He clearly thought that was explanation enough because he said nothing further.

At the car, the man looked to see if Victor had any luggage. 'No bags?'

'Just me,' said Victor, now wracking his brains to work out why the man looked familiar. 'I work in the Clanger Café. Do you go in there very often?'

The taxi driver held the rear door open for Victor to get in and hit him with a broad smile. 'Cor, yeah. I love a clanger. I think my favourite is the curry one with the mango dessert at the other end. Ooh, you're making me hungry now.'

A smile split Victor's face as he got into the back of the cab. The man had given him a satisfactory answer as to why he looked so familiar, but something in his head wanted to insist there was another reason his face stood out.

In the driver's seat, Francis turned the key. It had been even easier than he could have dared to dream. He even enjoyed acting the part of clanger lover, improvising on the spot to convince his first target. With

152

Victor Harris secure on the back seat – where he had already activated the child-locks and window lockouts to ensure he could not escape – he could drive him to the edge of town and get his phone. With that, because he felt sure the two targets were communicating with each other, he could lure the old man away from his dog. It was only late morning, his work was fifty percent done, and he could almost count the million pounds he would get when he delivered them both to the earl.

Looking out of the window, Victor shook his head. This wasn't the way to the police station. He opened his mouth to say something but that was when it hit him. The taxi driver wasn't lying about coming into the café; he'd sat by the window for hours a few days ago. Victor could remember the staff talking about it because there were two of them, one wearing what was almost an army uniform and the other … his eyes snapped up to look at the driver via his rear-view mirror. He hadn't seen him last night, but he was the man sat in the café with the attacker he did get to see.

Francis felt as much as saw his target stiffen and reacted by flooring the accelerator. They were coming out of the residential area anyway. He'd been made, but it didn't matter. He was always going to have to reveal himself to get the job done and now it was time to put his hardware purchases to good use.

Bluff

Albert left the dogs under the table when he shuffled off to use the gents. It was a risky thing to do because he knew Rex could easily drag the table his lead was hooked around clear across the café if he chose to.

Mercifully, neither dog had moved a muscle in the time he was gone. They appeared to be in some kind of food coma and, when he looked, it appeared they both had rather full and contented bellies.

'I guess you didn't need breakfast, after all,' he commented to himself. With a mental note to give Rex a lighter portion of food for the next few meals and abstain from offering him treats in the pub, Albert wondered if he should wait at the café or take a wander back to his accommodation at the pub.

Time was beginning to slip away from him and that created a new problem. He would be dissatisfied if he failed to clear Kate's name and identify the real killers, but he was due to meet Gary in York just twenty-four hours from now. If he didn't leave tomorrow morning after breakfast, his son would find himself there alone. It would be unfair to cancel and unfair to not be there waiting, but how could he leave when he suspected the remaining one of the pair who tried to snatch Victor last night was still in town? The only reason for the would-be kidnapper to still be here was to make another attempt and that made no sense at all.

It was about the hundredth time he'd gone around the same conundrum.

Putting his phone away, he decided to wander across to the police station. It wasn't all that far to go, and he could leave a message for DS Craig plus check to see if Victor had finished giving his statement. He'd been sitting in the café for hours …

The sudden flash of information made Albert jerk in shock. He only caught a brief glimpse of the men last night. They were both framed in the light coming from the inside of the van. With the rain lashing down, it had been about the only illumination in the dark courtyard, but it was enough to give Albert an impression of their faces. Only now had his spotty memory provided a link to where he had seen them before. He hadn't even realised that he had until now, but they were at the table by the door two days ago when the police came in to arrest Kate. He'd even spoken to them because Rex found a crumb of something under their table.

One of them was dead; the smartly dressed one, Albert thought. Which meant the one wearing army clothes was still at large. Maybe Albert would be able to help a composite artist create an image. He closed his eyes and thought about the man's features, but his concentration was interrupted by his phone beeping.

He had a text message from Victor.

Thumbing the button to show him the message, he then had to dig around in his pockets for his reading glasses. The process of patting down his jacket and then trousers – where he would never put them – led to the inevitable discovery that they were, of course, on his head.

Sighing at himself, he slid them into place and read the message.

'Albert, I just left the police station. They took my statement and asked me endless questions but now that I am on my way to the café, I just remembered something that I think might be important. Can you meet me? I can send a cab to pick you up if you like.'

Albert read the message twice. After the second time through, he looked out of the window and drummed his fingers on the table.

'Where do you want to meet?'

His response whizzed off into the ether, the reply from Victor beeping onto his phone only a heartbeat later.

'I'll send a cab. That will be easier than trying to explain.'

Albert thought some more, skewing his lips to one side and then the other as he tried to decide what to make of it. After a minute, he made a phone call. He was calling Detective Sergeant Craig, but he didn't get an answer from him. From what he knew, the man was heading to HMP Bedford to re-interview Kate Harris, the woman whose name Albert was supposed to be clearing. Albert didn't think he was doing very well with that.

Unable to raise the detective, Albert thought perhaps he could find a number for the local station. If he called 999, he would get the dispatch desk many miles away. His moment of hesitation helped him, for his phone rang the next moment.

'Albert Smith,' he answered.

The voice at the other end had a slightly bored and barely tolerant tone to it. 'Ah, Mr Smith. This is Detective Sergeant Craig. I have a missed call from you. I am just about to enter HMP Bedford, is this something quick?'

Albert frowned to himself. 'No, probably not. I think Victor Harris might have been kidnapped.'

Albert listened to a beat of silence in which he imagined the detective rolling his eyes at the other end. 'Oh, Mr Smith, and what makes you think that?'

Now Albert had to explain why he was concerned and realised how weak it was going to sound. 'I just received a text from him.'

'That doesn't sound very kidnapped to me,' DS Craig cut in.

'He's never sent me a text before,' Albert pointed out. 'More than that though, he wants to send a cab to pick me up. Have you had any taxi's reported stolen today?'

'Not that I am aware of,' sighed the detective, not even trying to hide his impatience.

'Why would he send a taxi to collect me?'

'Because you are old, Mr Smith.'

Albert had intended it to be a rhetorical question, but the detective's rudeness made him bristle. 'His text message claimed he had already been to the station and given his statement, but I do not believe he has had time for that. We know the man who escaped last night is still in Biggleswade and Victor's behaviour is strange.'

'Actually, we know no such thing,' argued DS Craig. 'What we know is that the person who forced Eric Simpson into the boot of his car returned the car to Biggleswade. He may not still be here, and he may not be the same person who attacked Victor Harris last night. What is it that you are suggesting anyway? That the same attacker has returned, this time successfully obtaining Victor Harris but is now trying to lure you into a stolen taxi so he can kidnap you too? For what purpose? Are you suddenly a celebrity target worth millions? Someone famous whose family will pay a healthy ransom? I think not, Mr Smith.'

Doing his best to keep his rising anger in check, Albert spoke calmly when he replied. 'Can you check to see if he has been to the station to make his statement, please?'

For a second, Albert thought the police officer was going to refuse, but with a teenager's sigh of open annoyance, he asked Albert to wait a moment. Listening to the hold noise, it took less than thirty seconds for the detective to come back onto the line. 'Mr Smith, the answer is that he has not yet arrived at the station. I am sure he will be along shortly. Now, if you will excuse me, I really don't have time for anymore wild conspiracy theories. I have a known killer to interview. Good day.'

DS Craig hung up, leaving Albert to stare at his phone. He wasn't getting any help from the police, but what did that mean? The obvious thing to do was phone Victor instead of sending a message. If he didn't pick up but sent another text message, then Albert would have his answer. However, as his finger hovered over the button to make the call, he worried that he might tip the kidnapper off if he was right.

'Why would he want me?' Albert asked himself, speaking aloud simply to orate his thoughts. Rex poked his head above the table, his tongue lolling out as he panted. Albert scratched his head. 'Rex, I might be about to get myself into some trouble.'

Rex tilted his head in question, looking at his human and wondering what, exactly, trouble might constitute.

Sucking on his teeth, Albert sent one more text message.

'It's a nice day and Rex needs a walk. I'm sure I can get directions if you tell me where I need to go.'

At the other end, Francis said some unrepeatable things and thought about hitting Victor again just to vent his rage. Victory was so close he could feel it. He had the original target; it had been unbelievably easy to lure the baker into the stolen taxi, but the cab's owner would have reported it missing by now which meant, in such a small town, the police would be looking for it. Maybe not taking it out again to pick up the old man was to his benefit.

Taking the negative and turning it into a positive the way he'd read to do in a management book on being successful, he started texting a reply.

'Yeah, sure. I'm sure that's a good idea. I'm in an industrial unit at the north end of the town. If you exit the café and turn left, you just need to keep going on the same road until you start to run out of houses. It's about half a mile. When you reach a big MOT place on your left-hand side, you need to turn left ...'

The instructions went on for a bit and were very precise. The message ended with advice that there was a lot of broken glass in the area and he should probably tie Rex up to the railing when he came into the yard. Albert felt sure it was a trap, but he was going anyway.

Meredith came over to collect his empty plate and teapot. 'Would you like another cup, love?' she asked.

Staying where he was to spend the day drinking tea sounded like a far better plan than willingly walking into an ambush, but if he was right, then Victor Harris needed to be rescued, and the man who had him was Albert's best chance to exonerate Kate. A bright spark of an idea ignited in his head.

Giving Meredith a guileless face, he asked, 'Do you have any teenagers in today?'

Ambush

Francis had a poor line of vision from inside the lockup. At best, he could peek through a crack in the door which was no good for luring the old man inside. His carefully crafted message to Albert laid the bait that Victor had remembered something he'd heard his attackers say the previous night and had followed it up to find the lockup. There Victor thought he might have found where his attackers had been hiding out; there were clothes and such, but he wanted Albert's opinion before he called the police. He told Albert in the message that he spoke to DS Craig about Albert's thoughts on the case and his sister's likely innocence, but the detective had been unwilling to listen. Victor wanted to be sure the evidence was solid before presenting it. Francis knew all about Albert, Victor's sister, and about DS Craig from the man cable-tied and duct-taped up in the boot of the stolen taxi now hidden from sight inside the lockup. It hadn't even taken that much persuading to make Victor talk, just a few punches and the threat of a soldering iron – another fun little toy from the hardware store.

Francis needed to be able to see the old man coming, that was what drove him from the lockup. Victor got another check and another threat. He was well secured; both immobilised with the cable ties and duct tape and also cable tied to a loading ring in the boot of the car. However, Francis felt it couldn't hurt to reinforce the concept of diabolical pain should he try to escape.

Thinking the old man must be on his way, Francis slipped out and closed the door, then stole across the yard to the main road where he could see anyone coming along the path toward him. Cars were going back and forth, and in the auto-shop place a hundred yards away, regular traffic came in and out. He had one moment of heart-stopping fear when a cop car drove past, but he managed to stop himself from looking at it and they just kept on going.

Two minutes passed, and in the distance, Francis could see a figure walking a large dog. It was the dog that stood out at first, but as they drew closer, the gait of an elderly gentleman became discernible and then his shiny bald head.

Francis pulled back, unwilling to let the man see him in case he got a good enough glimpse last night to identify him now. The next part was going to be tricky and required a little luck. There was no guarantee the old man would even step into the lockup so Francis needed him to get close enough that he could grab him. He also wanted the old man to tie the dog up and had gone to the trouble of taking out one of the overhead fluorescent light tubes in the lockup, smashing it on the courtyard outside to back up the claim that there was glass on the ground.

If Albert didn't secure the dog, it might be a problem. It certainly was a big beast and scared the bejezzus out of him last night, but Francis had a plan for that too. It is a little-known fact, so far as Francis knew, that while carrying a knife is illegal, a machete bought from a hardware store is another thing entirely. Considered a garden tool, the one he bought this morning wasn't the first in his life and being brand new, it was sharper than a politician's suit. It fit into a canvas sheath which was strapped to his right leg with the handle at just the right height for grabbing if the need arose.

Ducking into an alcove opposite the entrance to his lockup, Francis could just about see the street where the old man would appear. His heart was beating faster than he expected, given how simple this ought to be, and he put it down to excitement over how close he was to taking the earl's money.

Steadying his breathing, he settled in to wait the final minute or so.

In the street, Albert was feeling equally nervous. Wondering if he'd ever done something this rash before, he dismissed the notion of letting one of his children know because they would just make a big issue of it. They were all of a mind that he should come home already, and he'd called on them to bail him out in Bakewell and Stilton. Bail him out might not be the right word – possibly give a helping hand sounded better, but they had come to Melton Mowbray too, even though he told them there was no need. This time, he was doing it by himself.

And that was why he felt almost faint with fear. The man he was about to go up against was a big fellow. Not that a chap needed to be a bodybuilder to overpower a seventy-eight-year-old man, but unless Albert had this all wrong, the chap's intention was most likely to kill him as revenge for intervening last night. What else could he possibly want?

Telling himself to calm down and think straight, Albert paused just after the auto-shop. He could see the road sign pointing to the small industrial estate where he would find the lockup and that meant it was time to deploy what he hoped would prove to be a parachute. He made just one phone call, dialling 999 and reporting a break in at the industrial estate. He even gave them the number of the lockup Victor's text told him to go to, then cut off the call abruptly when they starting to ask him for his details. Then he set up his phone, repeating what Colin, the bakery trainee, had shown him how to do, and tested it before covering the final twenty yards.

Rex had his nose in the air, as did Hans who had been mostly asleep as Rex's human carried him along. Now they could both smell the man they wanted to find – the one who they had chased last night but failed to catch. Rex still wasn't sure what this was all about, but it had something to do with getting Han's human back and that was good enough for him.

He huffed and chuffed at his human, getting his attention. 'He's here,' Rex whined, puffing out his jowls in excitement. 'Just let me go. I'll find him and bite him and you can call the police. I won't let him get away twice and it's been too long since I got to bite anyone.' Rex liked biting people – bad people, of course, not just anyone, that would make him a bad dog. It had been his favourite part of police dog training; chasing and biting, although he got into trouble because he rarely bit the big padded arm he was offered, what was the fun in that?

Albert could see and hear the dogs when their interest changed. They were both alert, catching something on the wind that piqued their interest. 'Steady now, boys,' he soothed, patting Rex's shoulders.

In his alcove, Francis was getting agitated; the old man should have appeared by now. Where was he? He wanted to run out to the street to check but knew doing so would expose him if the old man came around the corner. It was a good thing he did wait for the next second the dog's head appeared. It was followed by the old man who was carrying the dachshund in his arms.

Francis held his breath and waited.

Albert wasn't sure what to expect when he turned the corner. There was no one in sight, which was probably what he should have anticipated – the bad guy, whoever he was, wouldn't be daft enough to expose himself. He had made it clear he wanted Albert to leave Rex behind with his line about the glass, but Albert could see something glittering on the concrete of the courtyard so maybe there was some truth to the lie.

Either way, he wasn't taking Rex with him. He had a better plan.

Rex was eager to go, almost straining at his leash as the scent became stronger and he could pinpoint a direction. His human's hands were behind his head; this was it; he was going to be told to sic 'em! Vibrating with barely contained energy, Rex couldn't believe it when his human stepped away.

'What? What's going on?' he spun around to look, his eyes amazed to see that his lead was looped through some steel railing.

'I'll be back in a minute, boy,' his human crouched a little to pat his head. 'You too, Hans. You stay here.'

'No!' whined Rex, tugging at his lead to get free. 'I can smell him. You need to let me get him before he gets you!'

With a final pat and check on the leads, Albert straightened himself and sucked in a deep breath through his nose. The lockup was ten yards away. He wanted to be sure the dogs saw which one he went into, which, if he had expressed his thoughts to Rex, would have made the dog despair because eyesight isn't the sense of choice when trying to find someone.

Francis wanted to jump for joy. The old man had bought every word of his lies. The giant dog was tied up, and he was seconds away from grabbing his second target. In two minutes, he would have two men stuffed into the boot of his stolen taxi and be heading out of town. He would stick to the back roads and country lanes on his way back to the earl, but he was a man who could get the job done and about to be rich.

Albert could feel his heart thumping in his chest as he walked toward the lockup. His legs felt unsteady, or less steady than normal which could be a little unsteady at times. How would it happen? That was the question pressing at the front of his brain. He was about to get ambushed, but would it be violent? That was the one thing he couldn't know. If the man hit him over the head, or simply wanted revenge and chose to stab him the moment he opened the door, then Albert was the dumbest detective ever.

It was too late to back out now and Albert had no idea how right he was to think that because Francis chose that moment to break cover.

Both dogs went berserk, which drew Albert's attention in the wrong direction. Rex was barking and bucking, tugging hard on his lead so that it bit into his throat and made him cough. Hans was no different, following Rex's lead in promising violence would ensue the moment they got free. However, all they could do was watch as the human they wanted to bite ran at Rex's human from behind.

Albert sensed him coming far too late to do anything about it, but he was almost at the lockup door by then. He turned just in time to face the man as he grabbed Albert around his neck. One meaty hand gripped hard and pushed him through the door and into the darkness inside.

'Whoa, easy, big fella,' Albert begged. 'I'm just an old man. I'll do what you ask.'

Francis had hold of the old man's neck and felt confident he could just crush it in his hand if he chose to. His job was to take the old man back alive so the earl could speak to him. Francis had no idea what that was all about, but the old man had no way of knowing his life wasn't currently in danger.

With a final check that they hadn't been spotted, Francis shut the door. The dogs were going nuts but by the time they drew anyone's attention, he would be in the car and ready to leave.

'Who are you?' Francis demanded gruffly, shoving the old man away. He knew his name was Albert but that was all he'd been able to get out of Victor no matter what he threatened him with. The baker claimed the old man was just a customer who popped in a couple of days ago and had been snooping around ever since.

Albert did his best to look terrified, which wasn't much of a stretch. 'Me? I'm just a tourist in town to sample the food.' The man seemed to consider Albert's answer for a moment. He looked like he might argue, but his surly face merely grunted his disinterest.

Backing away, Albert said, 'I came here to meet a friend. Are you the man who tried to snatch him last night?'

'What if I am?' growled Francis. 'It's of no concern to you.' He looked about for the duct tape and cable ties.

'No concern to me? I should say it is, young man. Where is Victor? Is he here?'

The brute's attention was focussed elsewhere; it looked like he was looking for something, so Albert seized the chance to get a little space between them, darting down the side of the red Ford Mondeo taxi. He wasn't sure what to expect but should have guessed the man would have stolen a taxi since he offered to pick him up in one.

The boot of the car was open, the lid held in the air under spring tension, and inside was the bound form of Victor. Even stuffed into the dark recesses of the car's boot and with duct tape wound around his head so it covered his mouth completely, Albert could still see who it was. It came as a relief because it meant the man hadn't snatched yet another person, but it also told Albert that Victor was still alive, a fact he couldn't be sure of until now.

Francis couldn't find the duct tape and it was beginning to annoy him. He wanted to get going. His plan was to immobilise the old man the same way he had Victor, but if he couldn't, he would have to settle for knocking him out – carefully, so he didn't kill him.

'What is this all about?' Albert asked hoping the man would reveal his master plan. However, speaking let the brute know that he had moved.

'Wouldn't you like to know,' he snarled. The old man was over at the boot now, which suited Francis just fine since he planned to stuff the man into it. That's where he'd left the supplies, now he remembered. 'Just stay right there,' he ordered as he started to advance.

Albert didn't stay though, he wanted a little more time and he'd already found the duct tape and cable ties just inside the boot, guessed what they were for, and hid them under the car. As Francis advanced, Albert ducked back along the side of the car.

It wasn't a game that would go on indefinitely, but he was desperate to get at least one answer.

'You don't want to tell me why you are kidnapping Victor? How about me? Why would you want to kidnap me? I'm just an old man on a tour of the country.'

'I told you to stay there,' growled Francis, beginning to get impatient. 'If I have to chase you, you won't like it when I catch you.'

'I dare say that will be true either way, young man. You're really not going to tell me why you are kidnapping a random old man?'

Francis got to the boot. The old man was now at the front of the car. He wasn't bothered about Albert's silly stalling tactics; he could catch him in seconds. First to grab the duct tape though. 'Where is it?' he roared while pulling his machete from its sheath as a display of what would come if the old man didn't start playing ball.

'Where is what, dear boy? You mean the duct tape? How about a little quid pro quo?' Albert watched the man's face crinkle with lack of understanding. 'Look, I'll tell you where the duct tape and cable ties are, if you will answer a few questions. I'm just curious is all. It's not like I can escape. I could never get to the door before you. It's my first time being kidnapped so I'm sorry if I am not very good at it.'

'You are going to make me rich,' Francis growled, finally providing an answer even if it was so cryptic as to be no use.

'Make you rich?' Albert repeated. 'How am I supposed to do that?'

Francis started down the side of the car and Albert shuffled up the other side. He didn't like the look of the machete the man held, especially not how big it still looked in the man's giant hand.

Francis grunted, 'You're a high value target.'

Albert screwed up his face in confusion just as Francis had a moment before. A high value target? What on Earth did that mean? It wasn't pertinent, but as he once again reached the back of the car, he paused when something caught his eye outside. There was a row of windows at the back and they were old, cheap plate glass. What he saw outside surprised him, but at the same time he also realised there was something he could no longer hear.

There was no more time if he wanted to get his answer. He stopped moving and held up his hands. Turning to face his would-be attacker as he advanced, Albert surrendered. 'I give in. I can't outrun you. Please just tell me one thing, and I'll get in the boot.'

'Where's the duct tape?' Francis shouted, pointing the tip of his machete in Albert's direction, and manoeuvring it until it was almost touching the old man's throat.

'Under the car,' Albert squeaked.

Francis gave the old man a hard stare. 'If you move, I'll cut off one of your hands when I catch you.' He held the stare for a two count, then got into a press up position to see if the old man was telling the truth.

With the machete wielding maniac's eyes off him for a second, Albert turned his head and signalled through the window. He wasn't sure if what he now planned would work but the police were yet to arrive, and he was starting to get worried they might not be coming.

Francis reached a long arm under the car, snagging the bits he needed before bouncing back onto his feet.

'Just one question,' Albert reminded him in a pleading voice as he held out his hands, wrists together, so the man could tape them.

'What is it?' Francis growled, tearing off a long strip of tape.

'What part did Kate Harris play in any of this?' Albert held his breath as he waited for the reply.

With the sticky tape held ready, Francis gave the old man a look that asked if he was suffering from Alzheimer's. 'Who the heck is Kate Harris?'

That was what Albert wanted to hear, but he needed just a little more yet. As Francis came at him with the tape, Albert faked a sneeze, jerking spasmodically and shifting his hands so the tape closed on itself and stuck together helplessly. As Francis growled with rage, and snagged the reel again, Albert pressed him one last time.

'She was the woman the police arrested on Tuesday afternoon. Don't you remember? You and your friend were sitting at the table by the door. The police think she is your accomplice. How is she involved in the murder of Joel Clement?'

This time, Francis stopped to look directly into the old man's eyes. 'She's not,' he stated. 'She had nothing to do with it. I killed Joel Clement, just like I'm going to kill you if you ask another question. Now hold your hands still.'

'No more questions,' Albert promised. 'Just a piece of advice.'

Francis had been just about to apply the tape to Albert's hands when he looked up in question. What advice could the old man possibly have to give?

As their eyes locked, Albert whipped his hands away, took a fast step back to the window and there he curled his right arm in so his elbow went high in front of his face and then extended it fast like he was throwing an invisible frisbee. With a barely contained laugh, he said, 'Duck.'

Rex exploded through the glass behind Albert's head just as he took his own advice and bent from the waist. Using the wall for support, he watched as the dog flew over his head. As a police dog, Rex was trained to do all sorts of things; jumping through a window wasn't one of them, but there were signals for 'quiet' and 'be ready' which he signalled through the window when Francis went under the car to retrieve the duct tape.

The frisbee move was just one they played at the park sometimes. His athletic dog was able to leap many feet into the air, and though Albert didn't know if it would work, with the police failing to respond to his call, he was out of options.

Francis had been about to grab for his machete and teach the old man a swift lesson when he saw the dog's face fill the window. He had no idea how the beast managed to get free and there was no time to find out. If he went for the machete, the dog would get him. If he tried to grab the old man, the dog would get him. If he even tried to close the boot lid, the dog would get him. All he had time to do was throw himself over the top of the car and get inside.

Rex landed in a skid, disorientated because he'd come from light to dark and because he had no way of knowing what was on the other side. He'd chosen to trust his human largely because he knew the man he wanted to bite was inside and this appeared to be the only way to get to him.

His paws were a little out of control and he had pain coming from his side and his front left leg. The injuries, if that were what he could feel, would have to wait for later though because he needed to make sure his human was okay and that meant subduing the man whose scent was in his nostrils.

The sound of the car engine starting told Rex he was already too late, but he got his paws sorted out and leapt for the car just as it sprang forward.

Francis was in a deep panic. What had been a perfectly crafted, seamlessly executed plan was going completely to pieces. He was going to have to cut his losses and get out of here right now. His door wasn't even closed when he let the handbrake go and stamped on the accelerator. The roller door to the lockup was down, but he figured he could blast his way through it if he tried. So that was what he did.

The industrial units were little more than wide garages with an extra pedestrian door at the side. Built back in the eighties, the contractor had taken every short cut he could because his winning bid demanded it. The roller doors were the cheapest things going, but at the time he'd managed to secure a contract to perform repairs at the building owner's expense and had rejoiced because he made more money from fixing the cheap as chips doors than he did from building the lockups in the first place.

Hitting it with the front bumper of the car did several things. Firstly, it folded the roller door outwards from the bottom which ripped the lower sections from the channel they ran in. Second, it yanked the whole assembly from the roof, exploding ancient, and cheaply made mortar which came away along with brickwork and the chain which made the door go up and down. Third, it set off both airbags.

None of these things would have stopped Francis from driving away, but the cop car just pulling to a stop outside did.

The two uniformed constables had been directed to investigate what dispatch thought to be a hoax call. They were duty bound to check it, but the level of urgency got dropped a peg, not only because it was likely to be nothing, but also because there was no danger to life reported: a break in at a lockup was not an urgent shout.

Constables Marin and Patterson had been attending to a minor RTA on the other side of town but were nearly finished when the call came in. Like dispatch, they expected it to be nothing but a hoax. Until the garage door exploded right next to them that is. Bricks, a large chunk of a galvanised steel roller door, and a bright red Ford Mondeo slammed into them as yet more pieces of masonry showered down on the roof of their squad car.

It scared the socks off Constable Marin who was in the passenger seat and took the full brunt of the low speed impact. Some choice words were said, but the time to gather themselves and work out what had happened was snapped away when the driver of the red car bailed out and started running.

'What the heck was that?' yelled Patterson. Then, when he should have been getting out and giving pursuit, he said, 'Hey, are you okay?' Checking on his partner who he'd been secretly admiring since they started riding together six months ago.

'Yes! Yes, I'm fine, just get going! I can't get out my side,' Marin despaired of her partner. He was nice enough but seemed far too concerned with making her life easy when he ought to be focused on the job. He was gawping at her now and she had to shove him to get him moving.

As they were bailing out through the undamaged driver's door, from the dark interior of the lockup a large shadow was emerging. The dust from the exploded roller door was still filtering out and shrouding the air in a hazy cloud and from that, trailing debris as he ran was a giant dog. It leapt onto the bonnet of the squad car to get around the wreckage of the roller door, and off again as he tore after the driver.

'Go!' shouted Marin, slapping Patterson on his shoulder to get him moving. Her partner put his head down to start sprinting but just as he did, something close to the ground and moving fast whipped by his feet. Momentarily terrified that there were terrible creatures escaping from the exploded lockup – Patterson watched far too many horror movies – he squealed and fell over. Marin's centre of gravity was already extended beyond her toes as she tried to get out of the car. Patterson was supposed to be gone, giving her room to stand and now there was none.

Falling on top of her partner, the pair got to see a pair of feet shuffle up to the boot of the red Mondeo and a second set of feet, these ones tied together in duct tape, appear a moment later. They were looking under the car, bewildered by what they could see and now they became a tangle of limbs and excuse me's as they tried to extricate themselves and get to their feet without inadvertently touching parts of each other they ought not to.

Rex knew none of this. He saw his human be grabbed and shoved inside the building but no matter how much he had bucked; he couldn't get his collar free. It was his new little dachshund friend who came to the rescue.

'I can gnaw through the leather,' he offered, putting his front two paws on Rex's neck. 'The lead is rope, that's way too hard, but I can get through your collar in seconds.' So that was what he did, using his tiny teeth to prove that size wasn't always the biggest factor. Once free, Rex performed the same trick with Han's collar except in his case, Rex just found the plastic buckle and crushed it in one bite.

Now free, the two dogs had gone to look for a way in. At precisely that time, Albert, backing away from Francis in the lockup, had suddenly realised he couldn't hear the dogs barking, howling, and whining any longer. He figured the police had arrived and were moving into position or something, but when a movement outside of the window caught his eye, a whole new plan emerged.

Less than a minute later, Rex was running for all he was worth. The human had a head start, but that wouldn't count for much: humans are rubbish at running. Rex suspected that was because they insisted on walking around on just their back legs.

He barked with joy, chasing the man yet again and feeling certain that this time he was going to get to bite some flesh. The bum was always a good target. It was at just the right height and people tended to be running away.

His own bark of excitement was echoed by one from Hans just a few yards behind. Rex turned his head to steal a quick look. His little friend was running for all he was worth. The bandage on his foot was half off now, and as Rex turned his head back to the front, he thought he saw it fly off into the weeds. They had reached the edge of the concreted area and were now on overgrown scrubland. The weeds and brambles, which must have grown rampant through the summer, were now dying back. They slowed Rex down more than Hans who was able to go under most of them while Rex was forced to go over.

Ahead of them, Francis was running in a blind panic. From the jaws of victory, he was somehow not only snatching defeat, but he was also going to get mauled by the dog and then arrested. He needed the machete. With that he could at least defend himself against the enormous hound. There hadn't been time to grab it though. At least, that was how it seemed at the time, but now he had to question if he had simply panicked. Maybe he should have taken the machete and killed the dog right there and then. It would have dealt with the issue. Then he could have vented his frustration at the old man and left without anyone knowing.

His scrambled brain had forgotten the police would have caught him trying to leave, but as his laboured breath threatened to overwhelm him, a glimmer of hope appeared.

There was a river ahead!

It wasn't a big one, but it was big enough. The dogs wouldn't be able to follow, and if they did, he could already see the far bank was too steep for them to clamber up. He was just going to have to jump for it and hope for the best.

He stole a glance over his shoulder, then wished he hadn't for both the giant German Shepherd and the daft sausage dog came bursting through the undergrowth ten yards behind him. Could he make it to the river before they brought him down?

Rex bared his teeth; this was it! He was two bounds away from leaping and could think of nothing other than bringing down his target, just like they taught him back at police dog school. Hans was barking something, but Rex's head was too filled with adrenalin to make out what it was. It sounded like he was trying to get Rex to stop.

Francis closed to within a yard of the river and leapt.

Behind him, Hans, who couldn't make Rex hear his message, ran directly between the larger dog's feet, tangling them deliberately to bring him down.

While Rex crashed to the dirt, colliding painfully with the ground, and rolling multiple times, Francis had a brief moment to savour victory. Then his eyes widened as he sailed out over the water and saw what was beneath him.

'What the heck, Hans!' barked Rex, trying to get back to his feet so he could follow the man. He couldn't believe it, he just couldn't. He was just about to leap when the dachshund tripped him. It had to be on purpose. Shoving off again to get to the water's edge so he could see the man and choose where to jump in, he stopped and let his jaw drop.

Between heavy panting, Hans managed to say, 'I couldn't come up with another way to stop you. I know this area. My human likes to walk along the river. There's a path on the other side.'

Three yards beneath them, the limp form of Francis lay half in and half out of the water. Protruding from his back, where it had penetrated his chest, but also through his neck, one arm, and both legs, were the rusted spikes of several old shopping trolleys. He was impaled and very, very dead.

Constable Marin arrived a few seconds later, whistling for the dogs in that ridiculous way that humans do. The dogs were still staring down into the murky water which made it easy for the police officer to find the man she wanted to question. When he leapt from his red Mondeo and ran from them, it was obvious that he had something he needed to hide. When the duct tape clad man appeared from the boot, chasing, and catching him became an imperative. That imperative was gone now.

A crashing sound behind her heralded the arrival of her partner Patterson just as she was lifting her lapel radio to call dispatch: this was going to take some additional people and resources.

Evidence

Sitting on the bonnet of the police car, Albert replayed the recording. Back at the café, a young trainee baker named Colin had shown Albert how to use his phone to make a recording. It was far simpler than he expected, and the lad had then produced a set of headphones and demonstrated how to connect them to be used as a microphone. In essence, Albert had created a wiretap to capture everything Francis said. He played it back for Victor and Constable Marin now with a satisfied smile.

When it got to the part where Francis confessed to the murder of Joel Clement and swore that Kate Harris had no involvement, Albert asked, 'Could you please pass this information on to Detective Sergeant Craig. I am sure he will find it pertinent.'

The young female officer had to show Albert how to transfer the file to her phone, but once she had it, the message that Kate Harris was indeed innocent, quickly passed up the line.

When she returned from the river's edge, she'd brought Rex and Hans with her. The dachshund was limping again, the wound on his foot open and bleeding once more, but he seemed to care not one jot. Rex had a cut to his right ear, another to a front paw and a small piece of glass embedded in his right flank. He winced in a high-pitched way when Albert found the source of the blood and pulled it free, but it wasn't deep enough to require treatment. He gave it a lick until it stopped bleeding.

Patterson had volunteered to go down to the body and confirm he was really dead and not somehow clinging grimly to life. Now back on the bank, and soaked from the thighs down, he waited for the coroner's team to arrive.

Victor was out of the duct tape and cable ties, careful use of the razor-sharp machete setting him free, but now they were bound in a different way – bound to answer questions and fill in all the blanks the police had.

An hour after Francis crashed through the roller door, ran away, and leapt to his death, a chief inspector from Bedford arrived. He introduced himself as Chief Inspector Andy Carter, a short Caribbean man in his early fifties with a receding hairline. By the time he arrived, a team of crime scene guys were doing things to the Mondeo, photographers were taking pictures of the scene and chaps in wetsuits were in the river with the body.

Albert and Victor were the centre of attention, as were the two dogs, but only because the chief inspector wanted to know what on Earth had been going on. Albert played the recording for him, the chief inspector listening quietly to that and to everything both men had to tell him. When they ran out of things to say, he wriggled his lips around a bit, totting up the factors in his head before asking, 'So what is this all about then?'

Albert and Victor both shrugged and the dogs would have done too if such a gesture meant anything to them.

'He called you a high-value target,' Chief Inspector Carter reminded Albert. 'What does that mean?'

Albert shrugged again. 'I really wish I knew. Killing Joel Clement appears to be a planned and deliberate crime, but possibly one which came about after he was kidnapped, and they discovered he couldn't bake. When he failed to do what they wanted, they came for Victor. Why anyone would be targeted for being able to bake a clanger, I have no idea.'

'This is bizarre,' the chief inspector commented while shaking his head.

Albert could think of no better word.

Cups of tea were delivered, and cheese sandwiches when they pointed out lunch had been and gone while they assisted the police in their enquiries. Statements were taken and the police had their contact numbers if they needed to get hold of either man again. Finally, they were free to go, but by then, hours had passed, the whole day slipping away in a boring manner which they were both fine by after the terrible excitement of ambush and kidnap.

Neither dog had a collar, so Albert improvised with a cable tie which served as a kind of macabre memento of their ordeal. Hans was bandaged again, a cop producing a first aid kit but advising the dog really needed to see a vet to be treated properly. Victor carried him anyway; it wasn't as if he weighed all that much.

On their way to the café, Victor asked how soon Kate might be released.

'If the police drop the charges? Straight away, I should think. If they accept the case against her has fallen apart, she isn't convicted, so they have no right or reason to hold her.'

Victor nodded. 'That makes her the new owner of the Clanger Café. I doubt that will fill her with joy given the circumstances by which she comes by it, but it is good news for the staff and the business. I think we shall have to organise a swift homecoming; I think the staff need it as much as she does.'

Albert nodded along. His adventure here was done. What the staff at the café might do and what might happen to the café in the future was not his business. In truth, he felt a little melancholy about it, but he wasn't about to take a job to become a part of their journey or buy a house nearby so he could see if they now flourished.

However, his belief that he was done, and his plan to shake Victor's hand at the café and carry on his way, went out the window when April appeared in the street ahead of them.

April

She was getting out of a car thirty yards ahead of them and was in her suit again. Joining her was a middle-aged man, also wearing a suit, but one that was very much more expensive-looking and screamed legal professional at a high volume.

Victor's stride faltered, but only for a second, after which it began to quicken. April spotted him and smiled a cruel smile as she pushed her way through the café door to get inside.

Victor rushed ahead, getting to the door ten seconds ahead of Albert and Rex. Rex pulled his human along when he saw where they were going. He'd had a busy day, and the café was a place he'd been given food twice already. It was getting close to dinner time, but he would happily fill in with a snack now.

Albert didn't need any more drama today, but he couldn't leave Biggleswade without seeing this through. With a reluctant sigh, he pushed his way through the door in time to hear Victor's cry echo out from the back offices.

'Unfair dismissal! Are you insane?'

Albert looked at Meredith, who was still working the front counter but now with a young woman he'd seen before, the one he thought was April's grandniece, Shannon. A quick glance at her name badge revealed that to be the case, but his focus was on the voices drifting through to the customer area yet again.

April's angry retort could be heard by everyone in the café; customer and staff alike. 'You see what I have had to put up with? The working conditions here are intolerable!'

183

Without asking permission to do so, Albert lifted the loose piece of counter. 'Hey, you can't come back here,' said Shannon, stepping up to stand in his way.

Albert paused to give her a hard stare. It was one he got to practice and perfect through a long police career plus fatherhood. 'I think, young miss, that you ought to come with me. This concerns you more than most.' Without waiting for her response, he stepped around her and let Rex lead him into the back of the building.

In the accountant's office in the rear of the building, the lawyer was laying out copies of preliminary paperwork. The firm would now have to mount a defence against his client, he explained. Albert stepped up to the door just as Victor tried to explain that April hadn't even been dismissed.

'There's no one here who can dismiss her,' he complained. 'She decided to take over and was trying to boss everyone around as if she owned the place.'

'Have you heard of constructive dismissal?' the lawyer asked. 'There is more than sufficient evidence to demonstrate that my client was treated unfairly and subjected to treatment likely to force her to resign her post.'

April shot Victor an evil grin and wagged a finger at him. 'When I get finished here, I will own the place.'

'I don't think so.'

The response to her claim came from behind Albert but he didn't need to turn around to know that Kate Harris was standing there: April's slacked-jawed expression told him.

'What are you doing here?' April stammered. 'You're supposed to be in jail. Why aren't you in jail?'

Albert took a step to his right, coming farther into the room which allowed Kate to enter properly and, in turn, reveal DS Craig standing behind her.

The detective gave Albert a stiff nod before addressing April's question. 'Miss Harris has been released and all charges against her dropped. I believe she is now the rightful owner of this business.'

'Ha!' shouted April. 'You can just arrest her again right now for embezzlement. I was going to let this drop, but now you force my hand. She's been fiddling the books for months, taking money here and there and covering it up with bad accounting.'

Kate shook her head as her cheeks coloured. 'You don't want to do this, April.'

April wore the smile of a shark coming up beneath a helpless bather as she relished the kill. 'Oh, but I do, Kate Homewrecker-Criminal Lowlife-Scumbag-Gold Digging-Embezzler Harris. I've got you now and you won't get away with it this time.'

Albert decided it was time to speak. 'I believe, April, that you have missed one or two critical factors.'

All eyes swung his way as he took control of the room. 'To begin with, if Kate is the business owner, she cannot commit embezzlement because it is her money.' April's smile froze in place and slowly fell away. 'That's fairly pertinent, one might say. More interesting though is that Kate didn't take the money. Did you Kate?' Albert asked, looking her way. 'Someone else did and you were covering for them until they could put it back.'

His final sentence was a statement, but it wasn't aimed at Kate. Nor were his eyes, which were locked on someone else's.

A tear fell, and the person looked down at the floor. 'I needed it just to feed the baby,' Shannon cried.

April looked shocked. 'No!' she said. 'No, it can't be you. It must be Kate.'

'Why?' asked Victor. 'Because if it is Shannon and Kate has been covering for her, it makes her the good guy in this mess.'

'And what does that make you, April?' asked Kate, a vicious glare piercing the older woman to the spot.

April's head was so bright red it appeared to be glowing from within. Her anger was at an incandescent level but got even worse when her lawyer picked up his paperwork again. 'You have deceived me Mrs Saunders. There is no case here at all.'

'They forced me out!' she bellowed.

He snapped his briefcase shut with the papers inside and picked it up. Pausing before he moved to exit the room, he said, 'I'm sure I would have done the same.'

A beat of silence passed after the lawyer swept around April and out through the staff gathered to listen in the corridor outside. Then with a weary sigh, Kate said, 'April, you're fired.'

April showed her gritted teeth, her breaths heaving in and out as she seethed with rage. Albert waited for her next torrent of abuse but instead she snatched up her handbag and wheeled toward the door. 'Shannon, get your coat. You don't work here anymore. We'll not lower ourselves to their standard.'

Shannon's head, which had been shamefully facing the floor, snapped up to look first at her great-aunt and then at Kate. 'Am I fired, Miss Harris?' she begged to know.

Kate shook her head. 'No, Shannon. We'll talk about the money in the morning and see if we can't find you a role that pays a little more money. Maybe you might like to be the firm's new accountant trainee.'

April glared at everyone once more, a look that ought to have turned them all to stone if they lived in ancient Greece, but she left without another word and when the door slammed in its frame, a spontaneous cheer rang out.

A line came to Albert's mind: Ding dong the witch is dead. He kept it to himself though, and when people began to file out, he gave Rex's improvised lead and collar a tug. Kate and Victor were hugging in the office, tears of joy falling from the new café owner's face as relief, joy, and sadness mingled and overwhelmed her.

A nudge to his arm turned out to be from Detective Sergeant Craig. He was facing Albert and holding out his hand to shake. 'Well done, Mr Smith.'

Albert knew this was the exact moment to rub the detective's face in how wrong he'd been. However, Albert wouldn't gain anything by doing so and that made it a petty act for a petty man. He gripped DS Craig's hand tightly instead, and said simply, 'Thank you.'

'How did you know she was innocent?' Craig asked, his forehead creased with curiosity as he waited for the answer.

Albert gave him a half shrug. 'It was in her eyes when you came to arrest her.'

If the statement surprised the detective, he showed no sign. He nodded his understanding, let go of Albert's hand, and left the office, presumably heading for the door.

Seeing Victor and Kate were still babbling about all that had happened in the last few days, Albert followed the detective from the room and wound his way back into the café at the front of the building. He intended to let himself out and quietly walk away but Rex's lead tugged in the wrong direction and he looked down to find his dog rubbing noses with the little dachshund.

'It was good to make a friend,' Rex admitted to Hans. 'I rarely see other dogs and most of them are smaller than me and tend to bark in defence.'

'Yeah,' said Hans. 'I guess I can see how that might happen.' All his own false bravado had been because the larger dog intimidated him. 'You're going now?'

'Looks that way. My human and me don't live anywhere permanent now. Every few days, we move on to a new place. It's good fun because everywhere we go, something is happening.'

'That does sound fun,' Hans agreed. 'If you're ever back this way …'

'I'll be sure to drop by,' promised Rex.

Behind the small dog, Kate appeared with Victor just behind her. 'Albert were you just going to leave? I haven't had a chance to thank you yet.'

Albert had been watching the two dogs but looked up to see the café's owner advancing toward him. He shot her a smile and gave Rex's lead a small tug to let him know it was time to go. Feeling like John Wayne, he said, 'There's no thanks necessary, Ma'am.'

'But you are the one who proved I was innocent. If not for you I might have spent the rest of my life in jail.'

Albert couldn't argue the point, not without pedantically pointing out she would probably be out in fifteen years. He smiled again and shrugged his shoulder. 'You were innocent. Helping was the right thing to do.'

There was nothing she could offer him that could ever repay the service he had performed, but she closed the distance to him and wrapped him into a hug. 'You are a special man, Albert. A very special man. If you ever need anything, no matter where you are. Just call and I will be there.'

A minute later, as Albert made his way up the road and back toward his accommodation to collect his belongings, he felt special. The day was already being replaced by twilight and if he were a younger man, he might have jumped in the air and clicked his heels together. Instead he settled for ruffling Rex's fur.

York beckoned. It was time to move on.

Walking away from the café, he felt satisfied that he had done the right thing by hanging around to unpick the mystery. But at the same time, he was perplexed by what he hadn't been able to work out. Francis confessed to killing Joel Clement, but why had the café owner been targeted in the first place? Why then had they come back for Victor Harris? Furthermore, who was it that thought Albert was a high-value target? He might have solved the case, but there was something else going on that remained hidden.

Thinking back to Stilton, Dave the daft security guard had stolen all the cheese, but he hadn't done it for himself. There was someone else pulling the strings even though Dave wouldn't admit it. Watching clouds roll across the hills in the distance, Albert made a promise to himself that he would take a broader view and see what else he could find. His children had access to the national crime database, perhaps there were other inexplicable food-related crimes in the recent weeks or months.

It was something to think about, anyway.

Epilogue

Several hours later and almost two hundred miles away, in a location that wasn't marked on any maps, Earl Bacon was not in a good mood. The late evening news was showing an article about a police chase and terrible accidental death in the small Bedfordshire town of Biggleswade. He already knew about it, of course, his B team were there to watch.

They were deployed the moment he got a sniff that Eugene and Francis might struggle with their task. His disappointment was such that he'd chosen to abandon his quest to gain a clanger baker. He suspected now that the delicacy might leave a bad taste in his mouth, much as the last few days had.

The B team, a man and a woman, were coming back to him, not picking up where the others had left off as was his direct instruction. The old man and his dog could be directly linked to two of his plans failing already, but in a moment of clarity, the earl let him go. He needed to focus on collecting the rest of his larder. There were more chefs required, more raw ingredients needed, and better security, that was paramount. Security was the primary reason he called the B team away from catching the old man. They could have taken him, but he wanted them to focus on recruiting a new B team now that they were suddenly the A team.

Savagely, he sliced into his thick piece of Japanese Wagyu beef prime fillet. He'd taken a herd from a town outside of Kyoto, using a team to steal over two hundred head of cattle in the night. They'd brought them all the way to his lair and snuck them in without anyone in the world knowing where they had gone. Two hundred head would keep him going for the rest of his life if the breeding program worked as he expected. He had two good butchers tucked away below ground as well as veterinarians, cattle wranglers, and a host of other staff to deal with all the foods he needed. He had to feed them as well, of course, it wasn't just him that had to survive.

That was his offer: the chance to survive the coming apocalypse. None of them believed him. Not one. He was saving them, but they cried about their families. When he started, he tried to calm them by bringing their families along: saving the entire bloodline, but they hadn't been happy with that either, so now he didn't bother. He was merciful, he was divine, he was the only one who knew the truth.

There was still so much to do, and he alone had the will to see it through. The old man and his dog were insignificant in the greater scheme. He just needed to keep that in mind and stay focussed.

Carving off another piece of his exquisite melt-in-the-mouth steak, he could feel his pulse slowing. Then an image of the old man surfaced again, and he stabbed his knife into his steak so hard he broke the plate in two. Screaming to the sky, he raged. 'There will be a reckoning, Albert Smith. I still want my cheese!'

The End

Author's Note

Good day, dear reader,

I hope you enjoyed this story. Writing this note, I am sitting on my couch with the rest of my family asleep upstairs. I assume they are asleep; I should say. My wife might be awake because Hermione, our daughter who turns four months in two days, might have decided she wants milk, in which case neither one is getting any sleep. And my son, Hunter, who turns five in just a few weeks, has his father's imagination, and struggles to sleep because he is battling time travelling alien robot dinosaurs.

Whatever the case, they are in bed, and I hope they are relaxed.

Rex and Albert are a joy to write, their adventures are just beginning as in my head I already envisage a second series of these books. Rex has a habit of waking me in the night, giving me daft ideas for story lines because he's got it into his head that he is the star of the show. Of course, he is right, but I can never admit that to him, his head is inflated enough already.

It is late summer here, where a heat wave of unparalleled intensity has dominated England for several weeks but may finally be over. There was rain today, falling onto my parched lawn where it will struggle to penetrate, and the temperatures have cooled. Yet despite that, it was still too warm for me to work in my log cabin.

I have several new series planned, my over-active imagination suggesting new ideas all the time. Some will make it onto paper, others will not, but those that do, ought to be crackers. Those that follow me on Facebook, Amazon, or via my newsletter will find about what is coming first.

I wonder did you spot the Blue Moon reference at the start of the book? The name Maddie Hayes might mean nothing to you, but growing up in the 80s, Moonlighting was the series that dominated my adolescent years. I have made a habit of sewing small Easter eggs into my books. Some get commented on, some are too obscure, but I wonder if one day a person will discover a pattern to them.

If you read the passage about Bovril and wonder what the heck it is, then your best bet is to perform an internet search. It is a beef paste which can either be turned into a hot drink or spread on toast. Oddly, I cannot stand the flavour now, but I ate jar upon jar of it as a child. I have employed the technique of plastering a blob onto the bath to keep a large dog calm in the past and will profess that it works very well.

Take care

Steve Higgs

History of the Bedfordshire Clanger

Bedfordshire Clanger gained a reputation as suet pudding (suet crust dumpling) wrapped in sweet filling at one and savoury filling at the other. Many people mistakenly considered it as another flavoury pasty, but it was different.

It first came into existence in the 19th century when the locals of Bedfordshire were trying local dishes from districts to come up with something new and thus Bedfordshire clanger was made.

From its early years, Bedfordshire Clanger intrigued the labour and working class in the area as everyone liked to hang out at a place where light food was served and since Bedfordshire Clanger was the newest and lightest of them all, it became an everyday staple of workers, specially labours.

Interestingly, the makers of Bedfordshire Clanger were women who first made this dish for their working-class husbands who, most of them, belonged to agriculture. In the 19th century, the mid-day meal was necessary for the working class as it came between their working hours or duty. Therefore, the wives were concerned about the diet of their husbands and thus brought this delicious dish to this world.

Today, Bedfordshire Clanger has become the symbol of recognition for Bedfordshire and portrayed as the 'defining food of Bedfordshire'.

There are different stories that history reveals to us about the name of Bedfordshire clanger. Some historians say that the word clanger referred to a word describing the mistake of adding two different fillings one sweet one savoury, but no one has come forward to support it with facts.

The most prominent naming theory that is most likely true is that the 'clang' means 'eating voraciously' in Northamptonshire dialect. It fitted best to describe the likeness of the 19th-century workers and was called Bedfordshire Clanger.

A similar dumpling was known in parts of Buckinghamshire, particularly Aylesbury Vale, as a "Bacon Badger". It was made from bacon, potatoes and onions, flavoured with sage and enclosed in a suet pastry case, and was usually boiled in a cloth. The etymology of "badger" is unknown, but might relate to a former term for a dealer in flour. "Badger" was widely used in the Midland counties in the early 19th century to refer to a "cornfactor, mealman, or huckster". The same basic suet dumpling recipe is known by a variety of other names elsewhere in the country; "flitting pudding" is recorded in County Durham, "dog in blanket" from Derbyshire, and "bacon pudding" in Berkshire and Sussex.

A baked "clanger" featured as a signature bake in episode 8 of Series 8 of *The Great British Bake Off*.

Recipe
Ingredients
The filling

- 1 small gammon joint (around 750g or 1.5lb)
- 2-3 bottles of cider (around 600ml or 20 floz)
- 1 bay leaf
- 2 sage leaves
- 2 apples
- 1 white onion, finely sliced
- 25g (1oz) butter (for onions)
- Pinch of salt (for onions)
- 1 ½ tsp brown sugar (for onions)
- 3 apples, peeled and quartered
- 3 tbsp brown sugar
- 10g (1/2oz) melted butter
- ¼ Lemon, juice
- 1 tsp cinnamon
- 10g Dijon mustard

The Pastry

- 400g plain flour
- 2 eggs, one for glazing
- 4g salt
- 130ml water
- 85 g suet or vegetable shortening
- 50g butter, chilled and grated

Method

- Place the gammon in a deep pan with the cider, bay leaf and sage, so that the liquid is covering the joint. Put on a medium heat. Bring to a slow simmer and cook for 3 hours. Once cooked cut into bite sized pieces.

- Place the butter in a frying pan and wait until it becomes frothy. Add the onions with a little bit of salt and cook until translucent. Once cooked through add the brown sugar and continue to cook on a low to medium heat until they are golden brown and caramelised. Turn off the heat and allow the onions to cool at room temperature.

- Place the apples in a frying pan with the melted butter and the lemon juice and cook until soft on the outside but still hard in the centre. Add the sugar and the cinnamon and leave to cool.

- Place the peeled and chopped potatoes into salted water and par boil. Then leave to cool.

- For the pastry, sieve the flour and salt into a bowl. Add the suet and the butter and rub in with your fingertips until you have a breadcrumb-like consistency. Add in the water and one egg and bring together. Once formed, make the pastry into a flat circle, clingfilm and place in the fridge to chill (if you're in a rush place the pastry in the freezer).

- Preheat the oven to 180C (350 Fahrenheit) degrees.

- Once chilled roll out the pastry, 2mm thin and cut 10cm by 15cm.

- Like when making a sausage roll, you only want the filling to cover one half (length-ways) of your pastry, so that you have enough pastry to bring over the top to cover everything neatly.

- For a Bedfordshire clanger you want the savoury filling to fill 2/3rd of the space and the sweet side to fill the remaining third. Place a thin wall of pastry at the two third point to prevent leakage between the two sides when you add the fillings.

- For the savoury side, first place a thin layer of Dijon mustard on the pastry, then pile the gammon, caramelised onions and potatoes on top.

- For the sweet side place the apples with some of the juices.

- Egg wash around the three sides and pull the remaining pastry over the top and seal. Egg wash the top of the clanger and place in the fridge for 10.

- Take the clanger out of the fridge, slash three times on each side, sprinkle with brown sugar on the sweet end and salt on the savoury and bake for 30 minutes or until golden brown.

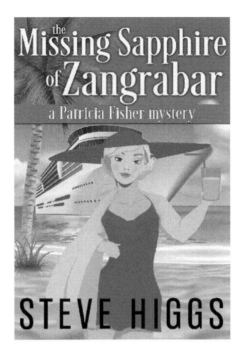

Read the book that started it all.

A thirty-year-old priceless jewel theft and a man who really has been stabbed in the back. Can a 52-year-old, slightly plump housewife unravel the mystery in time to save herself from jail?

When housewife, Patricia, catches her husband in bed with her best friend, her reaction isn't to rant and yell. Instead, she calmly empties the bank accounts and boards the first cruise ship she sees in nearby Southampton.

There she meets the unfairly handsome captain and her appointed butler for the trip – that's what you get when the only room available is a royal suite! But with most of the money gone and sleeping off a gin-fuelled pity party for one, she wakes to find herself accused of murder; she was seen leaving the bar with the victim and her purse is in his cabin.

Certain that all she did last night was fall into bed, a race against time begins as she tries to work out what happened and clear her name. But the Deputy Captain, the man responsible for safety and security onboard, has confined her to her cabin and has no interest in her version of events. Worse yet, as she begins to dig into the dead man's past, she uncovers a secret - there's a giant stolen sapphire somewhere and people are prepared to kill to get their hands on it.

With only a Jamaican butler faking an English accent and a pretty gym instructor to help, she must piece together the clues and do it fast. Or when she gets off the ship in St Kitts, she'll be in cuffs!

Pork Pie Pandemonium

Baking. It can get a guy killed.

When a retired detective superintendent chooses to take a culinary tour of the British Isles, he hopes to find tasty treats and delicious bakes …

… what he finds is a clue to a crime in the ingredients for his pork pie.

His dog, Rex Harrison, an ex-police dog fired for having a bad attitude, cannot understand why the humans are struggling to solve the mystery.

He can already smell the answer – it's right before their noses.

He'll pitch in to help his human and the shop owner's teenage daughter as the trio set out to save the shop from closure. Is the rival pork pie shop across the street to blame? Or is there something far more sinister going on?

One thing is for sure, what started out as a bit of fun, is getting deadlier by the hour, and they'd better work out what the dog knows soon or it could be curtains for them all.

More Books by Steve Higgs

Blue Moon Investigations

Paranormal Nonsense

The Phantom of Barker Mill

Amanda Harper Paranormal Detective

The Klowns of Kent

Dead Pirates of Cawsand

In the Doodoo With Voodoo

The Witches of East Malling

Crop Circles, Cows and Crazy Aliens

Whispers in the Rigging

Bloodlust Blonde – a short story

Paws of the Yeti

Under a Blue Moon – A Paranormal Detective Origin Story

Night Work

Lord Hale's Monster

The Herne Bay Howlers

Undead Incorporated

Patricia Fisher Cruise Mysteries

The Missing Sapphire of Zangrabar

The Kidnapped Bride

The Director's Cut

The Couple in Cabin 2124

Doctor Death

Murder on the Dancefloor

Mission for the Maharaja

A Sleuth and her Dachshund in Athens

The Maltese Parrot

No Place Like Home

Patricia Fisher Mystery Adventures

What Sam Knew

Solstice Goat

Recipe for Murder

A Banshee and a Bookshop

Diamonds, Dinner Jackets, and Death

Frozen Vengeance

Mug Shot

Albert Smith Culinary Capers

Pork Pie Pandemonium

Bakewell Tart Bludgeoning

Stilton Slaughter

Bedfordshire Clanger Calamity

Death of a Yorkshire Pudding

Free Books and More

Get sneak peaks, exclusive giveaways, behind the scenes content, and more. Plus, you'll be notified of Fan Pricing events when they occur and get exclusive offers from other authors because all UF writers are automatically friends.

Not only that, but you'll receive an exclusive FREE story staring Otto and Zachary and two free stories from the author's Blue Moon Investigations series.

Yes, please! Sign me up for lots of FREE stuff and bargains!

Want to follow me and keep up with what I am doing?

Facebook